BACK IN THE SADDLE

CYNTHIA TERELST

ISBN: 978-0-6487294-8-8

Copyright © 2025 by Cynthia Terelst

This book is a work of fiction. Names, characters and incidents are the product of the author's imagination or are used fictitiously. Any resemblance to actual events or persons is coincidental.

All rights reserved. No part of this book may be reproduced in any form or by any electronic or mechanical means, including information storage and retrieval systems, without written permission from the author, except for the use of brief quotations in a book review.

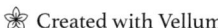 Created with Vellum

Some love stories have more than one beginning. So do we. It's never too late to reinvent ourselves.

Thank you for being here with me as I work on forging a new path. I leave a piece of me in every book. Then I find another piece to share. That's my gift to you. Pieces of me.

PROLOGUE

It isn't always one thing that puts an end to a marriage. It can be a lot of small things or a lot of big things. Sometimes marriages last a short time and other times they can last decades and sometimes they last forever.

Ciaron and Taylor's marriage lasted twenty-two years.

Their marriage ended in the middle of May, in the second year of the drought.

Ciaron was standing outside the meeting room interviewing a prospective employee on the phone for the upcoming breeding season. The lady was from Ireland and their conversation was in English, with some Irish sprinkled in.

Ciaron didn't miss Ireland; his home had been in Australia with his family for over twenty years. But when speaking with an Irish person, he just couldn't help slipping into his native tongue.

There was nothing unusual about the interview. It happened every year. Two new employees were required for night watch to keep mares and foals safe.

Ciaron didn't notice his wife watching him or her rising anger. If he did, he would not have understood.

Actually, no one would've understood.

They understood what happened next even less. Maybe they'd think back afterwards to see if there were any signs. Some thought there were.

Ciaron was happy with the interview, his last one for the year. He offered the job to Niamh on the spot. She would start in July, giving her enough time to settle in before the first foals were on the ground.

He was looking forward to the breeding season. Foals would bring much needed joy to the farm. The drought had been hard, and he'd tried to keep morale up. This would help.

Taylor didn't consider this when she stormed over to her husband. She didn't consider anything except for the extra wages she would have to pay on such a tight budget.

Should she have approached the whole scenario differently? Later, she would realise she should have. But that's the benefit of hindsight, isn't it?

Without that benefit, she yelled at him in earshot of everyone arriving for the morning meeting. And that fight was the end of their twenty-two-year marriage.

"Did you just hire someone?" Her voice was harder than a horse's hoof in winter.

If she had paid attention, she may have noticed him flinch. If she had paid attention. But that's hard to do when anger is not just in your voice, it's raging through your veins.

"For night watch," he said.

"We can't afford to hire someone. I'm trying to save my family farm. We can barely afford the employees we have."

He didn't hear anything beyond the words *my family farm*. At those words, the man who had only been angry a few times in twenty years, saw red. Blood rushed in his ears and to his face.

He breathed so harshly, it almost sounded like a roar, like a horse getting ready to fight. "Isabelle, Callum, me. We are your family. I'm trying to fucking save *us*."

She didn't hear. Didn't understand the words.

Neither of them saw the employees watching and listening. Rachel, the Foaling Unit Manager, ushered the employees into the meeting room, but they could still hear. Ciaron was talking so loud and fast sometimes they could only catch a few words, his accent so strong, uncontrolled.

Rachel was so shocked, she stared dumbly at the rest of the staff. It took her a few minutes to gain control of herself and start the meeting in Ciaron's absence. She did a good job not being distracted by the yelling outside.

Ciaron glared at his wife with the force of months of pent-up anger. "I've done everything I can for our family. Enough is enough."

He spewed out the words. All the words.

"I can't do this anymore, Taylor. I've tried." His fists clenched and unclenched. "You have no fucking respect for me or my business decisions." He looked around wildly. His voice getting louder, almost unhinged. "You question me in front of our employees. Our family is falling apart. It takes everything I've got to hold it all together. And you don't even notice because you're too fucking busy."

He realised she wasn't processing his words. He grunted, months of frustration evident in the sound.

"How many times do I need to fucking tell you we need you at home?"

The blank stare said she didn't understand what he was talking about. He threw his hands into the air.

"What?"

He made the next words as simple as he could. "I'm moving out. Our marriage is over."

And that was it. That was how a marriage ended. And the worst thing was, Taylor never saw it coming.

Hindsight is a bitch.

1

Ciaron

Sixty-seven days. That's how long I'd lived alone for, in this house on top of the hill, without my family, who lived at the bottom of the hill. If I lived for another forty years, I'd have another fourteen thousand days of this—emptiness, loneliness, whatever you wanted to call it.

More than once, I'd asked myself if leaving Taylor was the right thing. I'd argue with myself until the reasons no longer made sense. Had I given everything to the marriage, to her? I know I did, but then the doubt would start to creep in. Maybe I could have given more. Was it better to lay beside someone and be alone, or to sleep alone in a half empty bed? I didn't know the answers.

I stood in my kitchen and watched as the car's headlights shone up the hill and turned into my driveway. This was the third time this week that Isabelle and Callum had come over for dinner and it was only Thursday. Taylor must be working late *again*.

The front door opened, and Isabelle came in, followed by Callum. She looked so much like her mum, with her long brown hair, deep brown eyes and small freckles across her nose, but she'd never admit it. These days she seemed to resent her mother.

She walked with confidence, almost defiance. It was like she knew her place in the world. A year ago, when she was fourteen, it had been different. She'd doubted herself in every way. My heart lifted at how she'd turned that around.

"Hi, Dad," she said, parking herself on a stool at the counter. Her thick hair flowed down her shoulders, liberated from the ponytail she'd had to wear it in at school. She also made the most of being freed from her *restrictive* school uniform, wearing leggings and an oversized jumper with the quote *Stay Gold* blazoned across the front.

"What's for dinner?" Callum asked, striding into the kitchen and taking the lid off a pot on the stove. He was wearing shorts in the middle of winter and Ugg boots.

I didn't know that two children from the one family could be so different until I became a father. Where Isabelle was all serious, Callum was the opposite. Sure, they both had a great sense of humour, but Callum's seemed to be constantly there, evident in his mischievous green eyes and ready grin. Isabelle didn't let her emotions out as freely as Callum. He'd just say what he thought, with as much expression as he liked, and moved on. She was more reserved, keeping her feelings more to herself.

I didn't see that much difference between my four brothers. They were rough and tumble, loud and often antagonistic with each other, but not to me. I probably would have been the same as them if I hadn't been expected to care for them when I was a kid myself.

"Hi, Dad. How was your day?" I said to the back of his

head. His wavy brown hair curled at his collar. Had he combed it today? I didn't dare suggest a haircut. He'd probably shave it off, just to irk me. I'd leave that one to the school. They'd get on him as soon as it got too wild.

Callum ignored my sarcasm and turned to Isabelle. "Irish stew."

"Yum."

The taste of home, like my mam used to cook and her mam before her.

"I'm glad that you approve." I handed her three bowls and got a plastic container out so they could take leftovers home for Taylor. "Does your mum know you're here?"

Isabelle rolled her eyes. "I texted. Not that she cares."

"She's busy," I said, making the usual excuse, weak as it was. After all, it was her busyness that had contributed to our split.

"You work on the farm too," Callum said. "But you're never too busy for us."

My shoulders slumped. "It will get better after breeding season." I didn't know if that was true. Work seemed to consume her these past few months.

Isabelle scowled. "As if. Work is more important than us."

"That's not true." I needed to say more, but what? "The drought has everyone working harder." Lame, but true.

I turned my back to them and went to the pot on the stove before they could see my frown. It was one thing to neglect your marriage but something else completely to ignore your children, to make them feel unwanted. What the hell was wrong with her?

Isabelle was fifteen. She was becoming a woman, but she still needed her mother. There's only so much a father can do. But I was stretching those *father* boundaries all the time. What did I know about female body changes and periods? More than I wanted to. And Callum, he was fourteen. They say your kids grow up fast and they're not wrong. It wouldn't be long before they left home to chase their dreams.

"Isn't that why you broke up?" Isabelle asked. "Because she was always too busy?"

"That's between your mum and me." I stirred the stew and checked the lamb was soft. The children didn't need to know the many reasons why we broke up. All they needed to know is that it had nothing to do with them and that we still loved them. It seemed like one of us needed to do a little better in that department.

"Do you still love her?" Isabelle asked.

I stared at the wall as my heart squeezed. What sort of question was that? And how could I answer it? Truth was always best.

I turned to find them both watching me. "I will love her every day for the rest of my life." As much as it would hurt, I would.

They shared a look and smiled.

I didn't want them to read more into that than they should. "Sometimes love isn't enough."

I'm sure that statement went against everything I'd ever told them. And once I would have believed that love conquered all. I'd thrown everything I could into our marriage, but in the end, it had felt like it was all one sided. Taylor had not attempted to resolve anything when I left. She'd just continued on the same path—work.

I carried the pot to the bench and started filling up the bowls. The earthy fragrance of the lamb and full-bodied scent of the vegetables with a hint of fresh herbs filled the air. My stomach grumbled. "How was school today?"

Callum collected his bowl. "Good. Exams are finished."

"Holidays soon," Isabelle said, taking her bowl to the table.

"Parent-teacher interviews first," I reminded them.

They groaned.

Nearly July already. It was crazy to think that only a couple of months ago we had been all living in the same house, as a family. Two months since we'd realised it was going to be another dry winter, that we weren't going to get a reprieve from the drought. Two months since our lives had changed.

Drought was tough on farmers. Ongoing drought was worse. Every decision we made was stressful. Balancing the welfare of our horses with the needs of our farm team and the future of our business was a delicate act. Do we sell horses? Do we keep the horses? Do we reduce the number of client horses? It all needed to be weighed up.

We chatted while eating dinner and washing the dishes. When they were ready to leave, I gave them the container of food for Taylor.

"Tomorrow, text your mum before dinner time as a reminder to come home. You know how she gets lost in her work."

Isabelle frowned. "It won't make a difference."

"Just try."

I would speak to Taylor in the morning to tell her about the plan. That way she'd be prepared. It was a delicate balancing act—helping Taylor see how she was failing to meet the needs of the kids, and not pissing her off while doing it. Tomorrow's conversation promised to be fun.

"Give me a hug and kiss," I said as I walked them to the door.

"We only live down the road," Isabelle said. She

wrapped her arms around me, and I kissed the top of her head.

"I still miss you like crazy."

I pulled Callum in for a hug and a kiss.

"You'd miss us more if you move back to Ireland," he said, gazing up at me as he took a step away.

I sucked a breath in. Had Taylor said something to them? Did she want me to leave?

"Why would I move back to Ireland?"

He shrugged.

"This is my home."

Although the only thing that made this building a home was the children. Otherwise, it was just a place I lived and slept. There was no warmth, no photos on the wall, no personal belongings. I felt like a seasonal worker who brought nothing but their clothes. All my memories were in the house down the hill.

"What about Mamo?" Isabelle asked.

"What about your grandmother?"

"She might want you to move back."

She always hinted at me returning, but why would she want me to now, specifically? Had one of the kids said something to her? I hadn't told her that Taylor and I were separated. I didn't want to hear her say I told you so or it's time to come home now.

"I'm not leaving the farm. And I'm not leaving you. You live a kilometre away on the same farm and it's still too far."

I pulled them both in for another hug. Then I watched them as they drove their farm car to the house we'd lived in together until recently. The house I longed to return to so we could all be a family again. A house where silence was comfortable, not overwhelming.

Getting back together wasn't going to happen. Taylor

and I had been growing apart before the drought started a year ago. Then...it got worse. It wasn't only that Taylor worked all the time. She'd become less and less involved with us as a family. We didn't have any quality time together. Married couples went through this all the time. It happened to families we knew. I just never thought it would happen to us. And I'd always had full confidence that if it did happen to us, we'd be able to fix it.

I sighed and turned the lights off. Fixing it would only work if we both wanted to.

2

Taylor

I stared at the empty food container on my desk. It had been full of Irish stew. Did Ciaron cook it because he was homesick? Was he thinking of Ireland more now and thinking it was time to return?

When the kids had got home last night, Isabelle had shoved the container in front of me and said, 'Dinner from Dad'. He knew me well. He would have known I'd have toast for dinner. It was my go-to meal when he didn't cook for us. Until two months ago, that is. After he left, I'd tried to be better for the kids and actually cooked meals. But no matter how hard I tried, I still failed.

I grabbed my to-do list. It took up a whole page. I needed to go out and get some updated photos of horses and the grounds for our website. But none of the dryness of the drought, because no one wants to see that. I didn't even want to see it. Maybe I could Photoshop a green background in. With the coming breeding season, we needed to attract new clients. But I also needed to update pricing to reflect the current drought situation. I didn't have time for all that. I needed to enlist help.

I sent a message to Fran: You got a minute?

Within seconds, she was at my door. Her bright red hair was the only thing that brought light to the office these days. "What do you need?"

"I need photos to update the website. Can you send a message to the team asking them to take photos and send them to you? Once you have them, I'd like you to sort through them and send me the good ones. Then we can sit together and work on updating the website."

She nodded.

"After that, I'd like you to grab the expense statements from the last six months so we can update our pricing."

"Do you want me to ask Ciaron for help with that? He knows which expenses are abnormal and shouldn't be included."

"No. Just get me the figures."

She simply nodded and walked away. It's not like Ciaron cared about the business anymore. I couldn't ask him to help.

But...he had given the kids leftovers for me. So, maybe he cared a little. About me or the business? Who knew?

I sighed. Ciaron still knew me, but I didn't know who he was anymore. We didn't talk unless it was about the farm. Not even about the kids. We seemed to have two separate relationships with them. The one they had with him was full of love and conversations. With me, it was attitude and mostly silence. Like I was the one to blame for our separation, even though *he* was the one who left.

I flicked from tab to tab to tab on my computer, unable

to focus. I referred back to my list. OK. The next thing I had to do was look at the schedule of stallion parades to decide which ones I should attend in person and arrange for an invitation to go to our clients. At least we had a few weeks to organise that. Some clients enjoyed the prestige of stallion parades and would choose who their mares would go to based on the animals paraded in front of them. Others were happy to make their decision based on facts and lineage rather than be swayed by the stunning stallions.

My eyes strayed back to the container on my desk, and my mind returned to Ciaron. It was nice that he'd fed me. Or maybe he was pointing out how useless I was. Would Ciaron do that, though? Maybe. Probably not.

How did it even get to this?

For two months I'd thought about that as I lay in our bed, alone. I tried to pinpoint when it all changed and what, exactly, had changed. It's not like we fought.

I thought marriage was supposed to get easier over time. Like at first, it was all lovely because you were still in that honeymoon period. And then you started discovering things that irritated you, but you accepted them because they weren't enough to argue about. Then you knew all about each other's faults, but you were comfortable and loved each other and just accepted them for what they were. And then you got old together. It was at that last step we'd failed.

No point dwelling on it. It's not like it could be undone. He'd left, and that was it. He hadn't even said we could try to work things out. He'd made up his mind, and it was final.

I shoved my list of things to do aside. I wasn't going to get any work done if all I kept thinking about was Ciaron.

I picked up the container, crossed through reception, and went into his office. I took a moment to study him as he concentrated on the computer screen. The golden highlights in his brown hair were more prominent now than the day I'd met him, probably because of the Australian sunshine. And there was grey sprinkled in there as well. He wore it gracefully, like most men could. His shoulders, still wide and strong, drew my gaze. The shoulders I held onto as he railed me. The way I begged for more. How he made me come undone. I blushed and shook the memory away.

Everything about him was bigger, stronger, more beautiful. And I had no right thinking about any of them.

I strode to his desk and placed the container down. My forward momentum made it hit the desk harder than intended. I winced. Ciaron turned his attention from his computer screen to the container and then to me.

"Thank you for dinner," I said.

"No problem." He smiled, small, the smile not reaching his green eyes. On the day we met, those green eyes sparkled with mischief. I hadn't seen that sparkle for a very long time. Was it as dead as our marriage? If anything, one would hope being separated would make him come alive again.

His small smile disappeared. "The kids said they'd text you tonight before dinner. They reckon it's your turn to cook for me. You can bring me leftovers for lunch tomorrow." The lightness in his voice was forced.

I clenched my teeth and stared at him, willing myself to be calm. "I don't need you to remind me of my failures."

The fact that Isabelle and Callum hadn't been at home when I'd got there last night was evidence enough. I doubt the only reason they went to his house was for the food.

Ciaron raised his eyebrows. Was he looking for a fight?

Calm. I needed to stay calm.

I crossed my arms. "I wouldn't have to cook dinner if you hadn't left us."

Yep, willing myself to be calm had worked so well.

Ciaron broke eye contact with me, picked up the container and put it next to his. I took a tiny step back and looked down at my feet. What was I doing? I'd come here to thank him, not blame him for our breakup. Ciaron was trying to tell me in his gentle way that I'd been neglecting the kids. Gentle, not accusing. Well, maybe accusing. I don't fucking know.

"When did we stop communicating?" I asked.

"When you stopped listening," he said in a resigned tone.

It was back to being my fault again.

"Maybe you should have listened to my silence," I snapped.

"Like that even makes sense."

I sighed. There was no point to this conversation. It was getting me nowhere.

"Spag bol OK?" I asked. It was one of a handful of things I did well.

"I love spag bol."

I nodded and went back to my office. Why was I such an arsehole? Because he was better at this single parent shit than I was? I should be grateful for the kids' sake that he was. But the selfish me wanted the kids to be angry with him, just a little, for leaving us.

I stared out the window to what should be a lush, manicured lawn, but was now patchy and green-brown under the dull winter sun. I could see most of the paddocks from my window and the colours varied from brown to green the closer they got to the river. This drought felt like it was going on forever.

It had hit the Hunter Valley hard. All the predictions said we were supposed to get rain this autumn. It hadn't happened. And now the forecasters said it wouldn't. No rain meant no grass in the paddocks. We irrigated as much as we could, but no rain also meant reduced water allocations. No grass meant that we had to buy hay and feed for the horses. And just like everything else during a drought, horse feed was more expensive, due to high demand and limited availability. We were lucky that the larger studs in the area grew their own hay and sold it to the smaller studs at a discounted price.

The winter gloom had not only settled into the sky, but my heart as well. The feed bills had been piling up over the past few months. I was forever juggling feed bills, payments from clients, wages and vet bills.

I sighed and looked at the bank balance. Wages needed to be paid first. Our employees needed to eat and live. Soon, we'd also be paying the two new employees Ciaron had hired for the breeding season.

I closed my eyes as I remembered the rip-roaring argument we'd had about it. I'd never seen Ciaron so angry in all our years together. He was yelling and talking at such speed even I had trouble understanding him with his accent. That argument put an end to our twenty-year marriage. Twenty years of commitment gone just like that. It was probably a miracle it hadn't happened sooner. It was inevitable, really.

The same thing had happened to my parents.

My father's prediction about our love drying up and Ciaron returning to Ireland echoed in my brain. The fantasy lasted longer than he could have expected. Longer than his did with Mum.

The two-way crackled. "Ciaron, are you on channel?" Rachel, the Foaling Unit Manager, said.

"Yes."

"Can you come down to River Paddock, please? Dior is acting strange."

"Be there soon."

Acting strange in what way? Dior was our Group Two winning mare. It was only the end of June, so she shouldn't be in labour yet. The first foals wouldn't be on the ground until August. I checked the Repro App on my phone to confirm her due date. She wasn't due until 20 August.

Maybe she had colic. Should I join Ciaron to see what was wrong? She was an important horse for the farm and so was her foal. No. One of the things he'd said to me during that fight was that I didn't trust him. I did trust him. I needed to prove that by letting him handle this himself. He was Broodmare Manager for a reason. He was good at his job, smart and would be able to handle just about any situation without me.

I stood at the window and watched Ciaron drive to the River Paddock, dust trailing behind him until he was out of view. Then I waited in the silence that ensued.

I couldn't see all 2000 acres of our property from the office. What I could see were the foaling unit to the left, the hospital barn to the right and paddocks which stretched all the way to the river with post and rail fencing. Housing was interspersed among that space. Usually four houses or units together, except for our house and Mum's house, we had our own space and privacy.

Silence always made the thoughts lonelier. Or me lonelier. I don't know when I started undermining Ciaron and I don't know why. I trusted this man with my heart, yet I didn't trust him to make decisions in the business? He'd even been right about hiring night watch staff. We couldn't stretch our limited staff to cover the night watch as well.

Mares gave birth mostly at night and having reduced staff would put them and the foals in danger.

"Taylor," Ciaron said over the two-way. "I need you down here."

Shit. This wasn't good. I spun away from the window, rushed through the office and jumped in my car.

3

Ciaron

Rachel and I stood by the gate. Dior was fifty metres away, laying on the ground kicking her belly and rolling. She looked like she was colicking. Or maybe the foal was sitting in the wrong spot, making her uncomfortable.

"I'll get the kit out of my car," I said to Rachel.

I hurried to the car and grabbed my first aid box. We'd need to check her respiration, heartbeat and temperature. That would give us some indication of what we were dealing with. The best outcome would be the foal making her uncomfortable and Dior moving it back into a better spot. Colic could be complicated, especially at her stage of pregnancy.

Rachel and I approached the mare slowly. We didn't want to startle her or stress her out. Before we reached her, she stood up and pawed at something on the ground. My heart sank as an unmoving foal, encased in a white bag, came into view. Dior stood over it, her head down, nudging it with her nose.

We stood next to her and stared down at the deceased foal. We couldn't see the aborted foal clearly through the translucent white bag. It was brown like Dior. Quite large, probably 30 kilograms, which would be normal at this stage of her pregnancy. I crouched to get a better look. The foal appeared to be fully formed. There was a head and four legs, and it didn't look abnormal.

A car stopped outside the paddock. I stood and turned as Taylor approached the gate and looked at me expectantly.

I shook my head. "Stay there. She's aborted."

Her shoulders sagged. "I'll call the vet." She walked back up to the road, her head hanging low, to make the call.

I took a deep breath and turned to Rachel. She'd been on the farm a few years now, but even so, an aborted foal could still be traumatic. It was for me.

"Are you OK?" I asked.

She nodded. "There's nothing we could have done. Mares abort for a reason."

Her pragmatism reminded me of Taylor.

"I know, but I feel sad for her," I said.

"Me too."

I gave her shoulder a squeeze.

"Ciaron," Taylor called. She dropped two body bags inside the gate for the foetus. It would need to be double bagged to prevent leakage before it went to the vet for a necropsy. "Dan is on his way."

When I reached her side, I said, "From what I can see, the foetus is fully formed."

"Anything could have caused it. Placentitis, equine herpesvirus, some sort of deformity."

EHV was an infectious and notifiable disease. Precautions needed to be taken; we couldn't have it spreading.

I glanced at the other horses in the paddock. "We need to isolate the paddock. Can you remind everyone of the protocol at the afternoon meeting?"

"Yes. Salty is coming with the truck, so you can take Dior to the isolation yard for the vet."

I nodded. Moving her by truck would prevent spread. Dan would scan her and flush her to make sure she hadn't retained any placenta. He'd take bloods to test for EHV, progesterone and other important stats. For two weeks, while we waited for the necropsy results, she would need to stay isolated and would probably be on antibiotics.

We kept to the facts of the situation while my insides were reeling. Dior standing over her foal and mourning it was hard enough. But the fact that we'd lost a valuable foal was a big hit to the farm. Taylor would know it too. This was a bad situation in the best of years, but during a drought, it was ten times worse.

The afternoon would be busy for me, which was good; I'd need distracting. Helping the vet, disinfecting the truck from top to bottom, showering and washing my clothes. Later, it would really hit; then, I'd miss my family the most. Their presence alone would have helped soothe my melancholy. And talking it through with Taylor would have helped ease the worry. Instead, I'd be facing it alone.

I PUT my freshly washed clothes in the dryer and turned to go inside as the kids pulled into the driveway. Surely Taylor had got my hint about having dinner with them.

Isabelle got out and came over to me. "Mum told us to come and get you for dinner."

"I'm good. I've got leftovers."

"She's not going to take no for an answer."

I glanced at Callum in the car. He was watching us intently. I returned my focus to Isabelle. "Is that why she sent both of you?"

Isabelle nodded. "She told us about Dior."

"OK." There was no point arguing. The kids wouldn't leave unless I went with them.

They waited for me while I turned the lights off and then we headed home. Their home. Not mine anymore. Yet Taylor had still invited me in. She knew I'd be feeling down about the loss of the foal. Dior was probably over it by now and here I was still feeling sad. Horses are not like humans. I'd seen horses abort foals and simply walk away.

I wiped my sweaty palms on my pants before I walked into the house. I glanced around. Everything was still the same, except now the hooks were empty of my hat and coats.

Taylor's brown eyes met mine as I stepped into the living room. A small smile turned her lips up. My steps faltered. The smile may have been small, but it conveyed so much— understanding, acceptance, love. What was wrong with me? It didn't say any of that at all. It was a smile, nothing more, nothing less. Maybe she felt guilty about blaming me for her failures or this morning, where apparently everything was my fault.

Maybe it wasn't even her idea that I come over for dinner. I needed to stop wishing, hoping, for us to get back together because it wasn't going to happen. And making shit up in my head wasn't helping.

"I thought since you love my spag bol so much, you

should join us for dinner," Taylor said as she served out the spaghetti and topped it with Bolognese sauce.

My heart stuttered. So, it was her idea, after all.

"No better way to have it than with good company," I said. Was that too much? Geez, why was I overthinking everything?

The day I'd first seen her, there had been no overthinking involved. All I wanted to do was keep the beauty with wistful brown eyes in my sights.

I crossed over the Grattan Bridge. It was early afternoon, so the traffic on the road beside me wasn't hectic. Usually, I'd be rushing to get home before my brothers finished school, but Mam told me this morning that she'd be home. So, when my boss asked me to make a delivery across the river it was no problem. It was a nice change not having to hurry from my shift at the pub.

Voices drifted up from the Liffey River below. I looked over the railing. Some kayakers were approaching, drifting on the water as a guide pointed out buildings. One lass, with an olive woollen hat pulled over her ears, was a short distance away from the main group. Long brown hair flowed down her back. While the others smiled and laughed at the guide, her face was impassive as she gazed out to the old brown, red, and cream brick buildings four to five storeys high.

She drifted towards the bridge, closer and closer. My stomach felt like it was floating. I couldn't drag my eyes away. She was stunning. Her skin was tanned and small freckles splattered across her nose and cheeks. Thick eyelashes encircled her brown eyes.

The kayaks disappeared beneath me. I rushed across the bridge and made my way to the boardwalk, keeping the kayaks in sight as I strode across the wooden walkway in the direction they were heading.

People were sitting and drinking coffee in the sunshine, just colours as I dashed past them to get to the next bridge. I needed to see her again. I wanted to memorise every part of her, take a catalogue of all her beautiful features.

I was fortunate that not much paddling was going on from the kayakers. I was able to catch up and made it to the Millennium Bridge before they passed. I sent a silent mantra out, look up, look up, *begging for her to look up and see me, to meet my gaze, to smile only for me. Her gazed wandered everywhere but in my direction.*

They drifted past again towards the Ha' Penny Bridge and I repeated the exercise. My fingers grazed the love locks attached to the railings as I held onto the balustrade, studying her. This time, I noticed her full lips and how soft they looked. Her cheeks were red, probably from the cold. She wore no makeup, and she was perfect. Her eyes were what captured me the most, so soulful.

The group set off again, and I followed like a cat in the shadows chasing a mouse. The kayaks made their way to the boardwalk. I dashed to the spot, not wanting her to disembark and disappear. No way in hell that was happening.

I SHOOK the memory away as I glanced at Taylor, who was as beautiful and poignant as that first day I'd laid eyes on her. One look at her and I had been hypnotised. I'd never in my life looked at a woman like I'd looked at her, studied a woman like I'd studied her. I never would again.

"How's Dior?" Taylor asked.

"The vet didn't think there were any physical concerns. I think she's more worried about being separated from the herd than losing her foal."

"Depending on the results of the necropsy, we can send her back to the stallion when she's ready."

We wouldn't have to pay the stud fee again because we had a live foal guarantee. But that didn't help us right now. That foal would have been worth a lot of money and would have been future income for us when we sold it. It could have helped us boost the bank balance and help pay the bills.

Isabelle brought the bowls to the table. Callum poured some wine for Taylor and me. Taylor's favourite—a sparkling rosé from Hollydene. She must have found it stored away in the cupboard. A reminder of drought free years gone by. We sat down to eat. I tapped my foot in the silence. I didn't want to talk about work or the farm. But what else was there to talk about these days? I couldn't remember the last time we had an actual conversation. The kids were the most common ground.

"Callum and Isabelle have their parent-teacher interviews tomorrow," I said.

Taylor's brown eyes widened. "Did I miss the email?"

"It came out a couple of weeks ago." But obviously she'd been too busy to read it. I trapped my tongue behind my clenched teeth.

"We brought a note home," Isabelle said, sarcasm layered in her voice.

Taylor swallowed.

"The first one is at 5pm if you want to join us," I said. I didn't think she would. The school stuff was usually left up to me. It had been a year or so since she'd been to a parent teacher interview.

"Yes, I'd like to come."

What? Really? I gulped some wine. And another.

Callum and Isabelle glanced at each other, unable to hide their surprise.

"Excellent. I'll pick you all up at 4:30."

I could have told her we'd meet her there but that felt weird. I'm sure we would be fine going as a family unit, even if we weren't exactly a family anymore. And it's not like we argued...much. To argue, we would actually have to speak to each other. And we hadn't really done that since my big blow up. Most of the time she gave me the silent treatment, like I wasn't even worth the effort of arguing with.

Either she'd be quiet at the parent-teacher interviews or she'd be polite and agreeable. Both options would suit me fine.

4

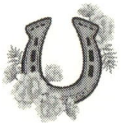

Taylor

I walked in the door at 4pm and headed straight for my bedroom. I needed to be showered and dressed in less than half an hour. I grabbed a newer pair of jeans from the shelf and a shirt to go with them. Were jeans OK? I didn't want to overdress for a parent-teacher interview. I shook my head as I walked to the bathroom. What did it even matter? It wasn't a job interview, and we lived in the country; jeans wouldn't be a surprise or unexpected. Besides, I wasn't there to impress anyone. Would Ciaron be wearing jeans?

I slammed my clothes down on the bathroom vanity. Enough with the overthinking.

The kids pulled into the carport, laughing and grumbling as they got out of the car. Isabelle kicked off her shoes as she came into the house. They thumped into the wall one after another. I smiled. Ciaron always told her that she'd be the one repainting the wall. Next would come...the fridge door opened—Callum wishing for some sort of treat to magically appear.

"Mum's home already," Isabelle said, her voice higher than usual.

I winced. She didn't even have confidence that I'd be on time for their parent-teacher interviews. I sighed as I hopped into the shower. I needed to up my game. As Ciaron and I had drifted apart, I'd drifted apart from the children. Why had I allowed that to happen? It must have made them feel shitty, and I'd never want them to feel that way. Lucky they had Ciaron...the Wonder Dad.

I shoved my head under the water and squeezed my eyes shut. Imagine resenting your own husband for being a good father. What was wrong with me? We'd become parents together, grown together in the role, supported each other. It's not his fault that I'd failed.

I hopped out of the shower and dressed. I brushed my hair slowly, killing time. As I walked into the living room, I plastered a smile on my face. "Are you ready?"

Callum looked up from his phone. "Yep."

Isabelle didn't bother giving me her attention. She merely nodded.

I tidied while waiting for Ciaron. Anything to keep busy and keep my mind off the distance between us, even though we were in the same room. I breathed a sigh of relief when I saw his car travelling down the road. I grabbed my bag and jacket and headed to the door, the kids in tow.

My phone beeped as I sat in the car. Ciaron's name popped up.

"The interview schedule," Ciaron said.

"Thanks."

I opened the message—form teachers, English, Maths, Science and Art.

"We aren't expecting any surprises, are we?" Ciaron asked Isabelle and Callum.

"It depends on what you consider a surprise," Isabelle said, a smile in her voice. "Callum, thinking lunch is the best part of his school day?"

Ciaron laughed. "No. He's been like that since prep."

"No surprises then."

We were quiet for the rest of the drive. Here, with the three of them, silence didn't seem so awkward. Not like it was sometimes if it was me and the kids. I needed to find my way out of that. I couldn't rely on Ciaron for that. Ciaron and I were no longer.

We parked and followed Isabelle and Callum into the school. I pulled on the hem of my shirt. This was the first outing we'd had as a broken family. What would people be thinking? This was a small town. Everyone was bound to know Ciaron and I weren't together anymore. I took another breath to calm myself and smiled as I looked around. Some of these one-storey buildings had been here when I was at school.

Mr McKinnon, my former maths teacher, and now vice principal, greeted us at the door and gave me a big smile. "Well, if it isn't Taylor Longmire." He faced the kids. "I taught your mum when she was your age."

He gave me a sideways glance, and I shoved my hands in my back pockets. What was he about to share?

"She was a lot like you, Isabelle. She studied hard. She never wanted to disappoint her parents."

Isabelle glanced at me. OK. That revelation wasn't so bad.

"But don't let that fool you. She was the mastermind of many devious acts."

Oh shit. I peeked at each of them. Their attention was held by Mr McKinnon.

"Like the time she convinced some senior students to bring sheep into the main building early one morning for the new principal to find. There was sheep excrement everywhere."

Callum's eyes widened as he spun around. "Mum!"

I shrugged. Ciaron chuckled.

"Ha," Mr McKinnon exclaimed. "I knew it was you." He guffawed. "Your mum covered her tracks. We could never prove it."

I elbowed Ciaron, who laughed with Mr McKinnon. It made him laugh harder.

I smoothed my shirt down. "We have some parent-teacher interviews to get to."

Mr McKinnon waved us through. "Sure. Sure." He moved aside. "I'm grateful neither Callum nor Isabelle have inherited your talent."

I leant towards him as I passed and said, "Yet." I grinned at his gasp.

Callum was practically bouncing beside me. "What other devious acts did you come up with, Mum?"

"This is not the place," I said, trying to hide my smile. I didn't know how I was going to get out of this. He would pester me until I told him something. The best thing to do would be to tell him the tamest things.

Ciaron moved in close. His warm breath brushed my ear, sending a shiver through me. "Everyone pays for their crimes in the end."

I whipped my head around to retort. My words stuck in my mouth as my lips brushed against his. They tingled. Ciaron stepped away, his cheeks flushed. My chest squeezed. Once, he would have kissed me right then and there. Now he wouldn't even look at me.

I turned my face and concentrated on the back of Callum's head. I missed Ciaron's lips, their tenderness, their warmth. The way that every time he claimed mine, I was his. I couldn't even remember the last time we kissed. And sex? That was almost non-existent in the months before our breakup. I needed to stop thinking about it. It didn't matter. He'd made up his mind, and I wasn't his anymore. It was only a matter of time before he'd return to Ireland and leave us all behind.

I couldn't simply will the memories away, because they were a part of me. Kissing Ciaron was a part of me, burnt into my muscle memory. It was tender and sweet, possessive and hot...

Ciaron wrenched me towards him; his grin and gleaming green eyes filled my vision. His soft lips enveloped mine, warming them instantly. Blood rushed to my head and then whooshed to my toes, making me dizzy all over. I wrapped my arms around his neck to hold him close and myself upright.

His strong hands were firm on my hips, securing me in place. They didn't need to; I wasn't going anywhere. My lips were willing. My whole body was. My tongue caressed his. His groan infiltrated every part of my body, and I held him tighter.

He grabbed onto my arse, pulling me against him.

The blood pulsing through me was slow, like a rhythmic, sensual beat, leaving wanting in its wake.

A small whimper escaped my throat and at first I didn't understand that the sound had come from me. The sound had come from me as I kissed a stranger.

I stepped away; our lips were the last parts of our body to disengage. It was like they knew other lips would never feel as good as this. My eyes opened to him, staring wide-eyed at me. And my lips that had kissed the hell out of him lifted into a smile.

I TOOK a ragged breath and lifted my fingertips to my mouth. I snuck a look at Ciaron, who stared ahead, not even acknowledging my presence. It seemed I was the only one lost in the past.

"We'll wait in the lounge," Isabelle said. As she and Callum walked away, they spoke to each other, continuously glancing back at us and nodding.

"Ciaron, it's so nice to see you again," a lady with long blonde hair said with a wide smile as she stood up. I was surprised she didn't round the desk to embrace him in her enthusiasm.

"You too, Carla."

Her gaze flitted to me. Her bright blue eyes were curious.

Ciaron took a half step away from me. "This is Taylor m —Isabelle and Callum's mum."

My stomach knotted. Carla wouldn't have noticed his little stumble. I tried to hide the hurt by sticking my hand out. I needed to get used to it. That's all I was to Ciaron now —the mother of his children.

"Taylor, this is Carla, Isabelle's homeroom teacher."

I nodded as we sat and twisted the Claddagh ring I'd never taken off since my time with him in Ireland.

She'd said it was nice to see him again. When had they seen each other? This was the first parent-teacher interview of the year.

"You must be so proud of Isabelle," Carla said in an uplifted voice.

Ugh...young, bright and cheerful. Everything I wasn't.

I nodded again. I was always proud of Isabelle. But it seemed there was a particular reason I should be in this case. I tried to wrack my brain for what had happened so far this year and came up empty.

"She has worked so hard this semester to improve her grades. Some of it had to do with choosing the right friends and some to do with the extra work she's been doing at home."

I nodded and smiled. It was the best thing I could do to hide my ignorance. I remembered Ciaron's words: *I'm fighting to save this family.* Was this what he'd meant?

Ciaron smiled at Carla. "I think it had something to do with your influence too." Then he glanced at me. "We are both very proud of the effort Isabelle has put in."

Carla beamed at Ciaron and continued looking at him as she spoke. I wanted to poke her eyes out with one of her pens. "Ciaron has been a Godsend. Isabelle is lucky to have such an invested dad." She faced me. "We've been working closely together all year."

Have they just? Is that why he corrected himself before he called me his wife? When he said we are both proud of Isabelle, did he mean him and me or him and Carla?

I couldn't form words. So, it was another nod from me. I forced myself to concentrate on the remainder of the meeting and the next and the next. Before we went back to the kids, I pulled Ciaron into an alcove along the hallway.

He had some things to answer for.

5

Ciaron

In the privacy of an alcove, Taylor crossed her arms and narrowed her eyes at me. "How long has this been going on?"

I stopped myself from letting out a huff. She'd been in a mood since we'd spoken to Carla. I'd told her about Isabelle on numerous occasions. It's not my fault she'd paid no attention. "All year."

"Do the kids know?"

I frowned. "Well, it's no secret."

She took a step back. Her breathing was ragged. "They know about you and Carla?"

I shrugged and shook my head. "Why wouldn't they know?"

"I don't know. Maybe out of respect for me."

She couldn't be serious, could she? One glance at her flattened lips told me she was. My vision blurred as rage pulsed in my veins. I dragged her into an empty classroom off the alcove. "What the hell are you talking about?

Respect? Your daughter was struggling and all you can think about is yourself. How about some fucking respect for her? Maybe pretend to care a little bit."

She glared at me. If looks could kill, I'd be dead. "It's a bit hard not to think about myself when everyone knew you were having an affair except for me."

I was ready to give her a piece of my mind about being a crappy parent, but stopped when I registered what she said. "A—what? An affair?"

"You and Carla."

"We're not having an affair."

"Then why did you meet with her?"

"So we could go through the material Isabelle was learning. So I could help our daughter. Something you couldn't care less about."

Taylor stared at me, her eyes calculating.

I matched her glare. Fuck being polite. I'd put up with a lot during our marriage, but I wasn't putting up with diddly squat anymore.

"The question is why *you* didn't bother helping our daughter? Oh, that's right, you were too fucking busy." My voice was raised, and I didn't care. I pointed my finger at her. "You think so little of me that you think I would have an affair?" I threw my hands into the air. "Even worse, you think your children would be OK with that?"

Taylor looked down at her feet. "No, of course not." She lifted her gaze. Tears welled in her eyes. What the fuck? One minute she was ready to kill me and the next she's crying?

"Well, you just fucking accused us of it."

"I'm sorry, Ciaron. I know you wouldn't do that." She took a trembling breath. "But I didn't think you'd leave me either."

I ran my hand through my hair. "I didn't have much

choice." My voice was calmer now. Surprising, since my stomach was twisted in knots and my heart pounded as I went from disbelief to anger to pain over and over again.

She nodded. Is that all she had for me? Was she conceding she was in the wrong? Did she understand why I'd chosen to leave? Here we were, back to no communication. A marriage couldn't survive like this. That's why it hadn't.

I was struggling; my fists were clenched at my side. If it wasn't for the kids, I would have told her to fuck off and walked away.

I ran my hand through my hair. If I didn't want the lack of communication to continue, I would need to do something about it, starting now. "I don't want to be those parents, Taylor. The ones who can't even be civil."

She inclined her chin. "Neither do I."

"I did try to tell you about Isabelle. But your focus was the farm."

"Yes." Her voice was barely above a whisper. Was this finally sinking in? If it was, it was too late.

"The kids are waiting for us," I said, making my way to the door.

Taylor followed.

This night wasn't about Taylor and me. It was about the kids. I moved what had happened to the back of my thoughts and smiled as Isabelle and Callum met us at the door of the lounge.

"Looks like I owe you pizza." I hugged Isabelle's shoulders. "You did it, kiddo." I grinned at Callum. "It seems that lunch isn't your favourite subject, after all."

Callum smirked. "Who would have thought a budding young scientist could come from you two?"

Taylor poked him in the ribs. "You know, producing good horses isn't just luck. There's a science behind it."

"If you say so." He walked down the corridor. "Pizza will wait for no man."

Taylor and Isabelle followed. I stayed close behind and listened as Taylor told Isabelle how proud she was of her. The perk in Isabelle's step was all the reward I needed at that moment.

The fun banter didn't stop all the way to the restaurant and while we waited for our food. I was grateful. Because every time there was a lull in the conversation, I thought about the argument with Taylor and what she'd accused me of.

"What are you doing in science next semester?" I asked Callum.

"Genetics."

Isabelle laughed. "You and Mum can be mad scientists together."

I grinned at Isabelle. "It would be a horse-dirt bike mashup."

She spoke directly to me like Taylor and Callum weren't even there. "Maybe a self-washing one. Then we won't have to listen to them complain about how dirty it is."

"And it would do roll backs, go at the exact right speed and jump on command," I added.

"My bike does that," Callum said.

"Myrtle does that," Taylor said.

Myrtle, Taylor's horse, did nothing on command. The kids and I laughed so hard tears were running down Isabelle's face. Taylor sat there stone faced.

I tried to compose myself. "Only if you don't tell her to," I managed to say between gulps of air.

"She has personality," Taylor stated.

"She's as stubborn as a mule," I said.

Isabelle said, "Don't animals take after their owners?"

The kids and I looked at each other and started a fresh round of laughter. Taylor's lips quirked. "Laugh as much as you want. But we all know Myrtle would beat your dad's horse any day."

This. This is what I missed. Us enjoying our company—talking and laughing together as a family. But even though I was enjoying this time together, it didn't matter. What had happened earlier proved that we were beyond repair. Taylor accusing me of cheating was a low blow. I would never cheat.

My father had been in and out of jail since I was a kid and had cheated on my mother the whole time. And she on him. To say that to me...to accuse me of that...my chest ached as another piece of my heart was destroyed. Taylor, my once in a lifetime love, no longer loved me.

She knew I never wanted to be anything like my parents. They didn't even know the meaning of faithful. I'd never looked at another woman after I'd met Taylor. I didn't need to; she was all I wanted, all I needed.

My stomach was as heavy as lead. Twenty-two years of our lives together and she didn't even know me. Either that or she'd said it to hurt me. May as well give me lead boots to go with that lead in my stomach.

I inhaled slowly to calm my nerves. I guess I'd had this sliver of hope up until that moment. Fucking hell. I'd even thought about our first kiss after our lips touched in the corridor. But no more. I lay my hands on top of my thighs to stop the shaking. Hearts break every day and people get over it. I would too, in time.

As we ate, Isabelle and Callum were having some secret conversation. They'd been doing that a lot lately. Is that something kids learnt to do when their parents separated? Perhaps it was a coping mechanism as they learnt to trust what their new life was becoming. Maybe they took solace in each other.

Isabelle showed Callum her phone. He smirked.

"Is there something you'd like to share with us?" I asked.

"You'll find out soon enough," Isabelle said.

I did not like the sound of that. Their coping mechanism better not extend to causing some sort of trouble as they pitted themselves against us. I was not in the mood for some kid-made war. I had enough trouble keeping my feelings straight where their mother was concerned. The roller coaster of feelings didn't stop once you said enough and broke up. I didn't know if it was ever going to stop.

I'd heard people say that you were finally ready to move on once you had no feelings left for your ex-partner. Those feelings could be hurt, anger, love, whatever. The feelings were exhausting. How much longer would I have them now that I knew there was no hope?

6

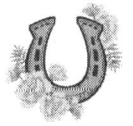

Taylor

Laughter filtered in through my office door. Ciaron and the woman he'd hired from Ireland were joking about something. Words were spoken in English and Irish.

"It only rains twice a week in *Éirinn*," Ciaron said.

"Once for *trí lá* and the second time for *ceithre lá,*" Niamh replied.

They both laughed...again. I think she said it rained for three days and then four days every week. Not that I was trying to listen. They were just so loud.

"How many in your *teaghlach*?" Niamh asked. "Are they all here in Australia?"

"Just me in Australia," Ciaron said. Did I hear sadness in his voice? No, wait—I shifted in my seat and rubbed the ring on my finger. He didn't mention us. Isabelle, Callum and me? We were his family. My stomach squeezed. Not me. I wasn't his family anymore, but the kids were.

She said something in reply that I couldn't hear. Then said, "*Cárb as duit?*"

"Sheriff Street."

"No *capall* there." She laughed.

"No, lots of people betting on them, though."

More chuckling, followed by footsteps. They were walking into the central office.

"Fran, I'm going to show Niamh around," Ciaron said. "Can you please check her forms while we're gone?"

"No problem," Fran said.

I half expected him to walk over to my door to introduce Niamh. That's what he would normally do. Instead, the footsteps faded as he led her outside. Good. I didn't want to hear any more of his laughter and fun. I didn't want to hear him slip into his Irish tongue like it was so damn natural, and that's where he belonged.

"Would you ever go back?" Niamh asked as they walked out the door.

I strained to hear the answer, but they were too far away.

Ever since the parent-teacher interviews two weeks ago, Ciaron had been distant. He didn't cook any meals for me and only spoke to me when necessary. He even avoided being with me and the kids at the same time. And in the office, he made sure not to be in the same room as me, if he could help it. If I was in the main office area, he would wait for me to leave before he went to speak to Fran. Or if he was there when I walked in, he would make a quick departure.

It was my fault. In that moment when I'd accused him of cheating, I couldn't see past my jealousy. The words had come out without me even thinking. Because, if I had stopped for one second and thought about it, they would never have come out. I would have known how stupid I was to even think them.

I didn't know how to fix it. I stared at the ceiling, like the answers would suddenly appear in the blank white space. The word sorry wouldn't be enough. But what would?

I missed him. Even though we'd been separated for months, it felt more final. We hadn't lost only our marriage, but our friendship and camaraderie as well. I'd had a glimpse of it when we were having pizza, but it had vanished as quickly as it had appeared. The ache in my chest doubled each time I thought about it.

I had so much to do and yet all I could do was think about him.

I watched from the window as Ciaron and Niamh hopped onto the buggy, wearing heavy winter jackets to ward off the winter chill. They were still talking and joking. When was the last time Ciaron and I laughed as freely as that? In the end, our marriage hadn't been about us anymore. It was about a million other things, and we were left like riders without a horse.

All those times I'd questioned his decisions, I never thought about how that made him feel. I never thought about how those moments would hurt him or how he would be embarrassed. I just thought about how he was wrong, or more like how I *thought* he was wrong. What does that do to the core of a person, when their wife, who should be their biggest supporter, is the opposite? It crushes them is what it does.

Fuck.

Add to that the lack of togetherness and intimacy.

No wonder he'd left me.

From my vantage point, I watched as Ciaron explained the lay of the land. He stopped a lot and appeared to give lots of information. When I couldn't see them anymore, I turned back to my computer and concentrated on investigating what stallions were standing at stud this year. Ciaron and I usually worked together on deciding which stallions and mares would make the best offspring at the price we could afford. Some horses like Cox Plate winner, Anamoe, cost $121,000, which was completely out of our budget.

Neither of us had approached the other about it. I opened my calendar and thought about booking a meeting with him. I sighed. Is this what our lives had become? Avoidance and forced interactions through meetings?

Ciaron and Niamh headed back up the hill. It was time for me to go do some rounds, better known as avoiding the banter and laughter between them. Something I doubt I'd share with Ciaron again.

I walked out into the central office with its four desks, fireplace and floor to ceiling bookcases. We were down to one admin person at the moment but would increase to another one during breeding season, which would start in a couple of weeks. We couldn't expect Fran to do it all. She was already covering two jobs with Ciaron and me helping where we could. We just couldn't afford another admin person full time.

Fran looked up from her desk. "Have you got a minute to discuss the fuel? It's not adding up for me."

I glanced out the window. I had five minutes before Ciaron got back. "Sure." I walked around her desk and stood beside her so I could see her screen.

She pointed with her mouse. "The fuel truck put 2100 litres in to fill the tank. These are all the entries from the book when everyone got fuel, they don't add up to 2100."

Ciaron and Niamh were still making their way back. With luck, they might stop to look at something.

"I've double checked all of my entries," Fran said, shaking her head.

I scanned the screen for anything unusual. Everything looked OK. "Have you checked if any of the usuals didn't get petrol this month?"

Fran nodded.

"Let me read the entries to you." I read the names and numbers out at top speed while watching Ciaron and Niamh make their way up the hill.

"Stop," Fran called out.

I reread the last entry.

"That's it," Fran said. "The numbers are transposed."

Ciaron pulled up at the front of the office. I clenched my fists. For fuck's sake. Fran said she'd double checked the entries. If she'd double checked, how did she miss it? I shook my head. No. That wasn't fair. We'd all done the same thing at least once. That's why we worked as a team.

I stood up straight. "Great"

Before she could say anything else, I made my way to the door. "Gotta go."

As my hand reached out, the door swung open. Fuck, I'd missed my escape. I stepped back. Ciaron entered, followed by Niamh. So much for avoiding them. His eyes widened as he stopped inside the door. Niamh nearly walked into him. Ciaron and I stared at each other.

He turned to Niamh. "Taylor, this is Niamh. She's joined us for night watch."

I shook her hand. "Nice to meet you. Welcome to Diamond Firetail Farm."

"Thank you."

I stared at him. My heartbeat galloped as I waited to see how he was going to introduce me. He couldn't refer to me as the kids' mother this time.

"Taylor is my partner. She is the general manager."

My stomach plummeted. He'd intentionally called me

partner, not even stumbling on the word. How long had he been thinking of a way to introduce me? I forced my shoulders to stay high and my chin elevated. Then I moved aside so they could pass. "I'm needed down at the hospital barn. Thanks for joining our team." I hurried out the door.

Partner, huh? As in business partners? Like we both had a stake in the farm? This farm had been in my family for generations. *My family*. I had no idea what would happen to it if he staked a claim. I suppose I would need to find a way to pay him out, but in a drought, that would be near impossible. Then again, if it was valued now, it wouldn't be worth as much.

I swallowed the lump in my throat. Could anything be worse than losing my best friend, my husband, my family and the business?

7

Ciaron

I smiled, remembering the conversations I had with Niamh. The first one, naturally, revolved around the weather. Then where we were from. I hadn't met anyone yet that knew any people I'd known. The horse scene and city pub scene were two different things.

I never wanted to go back there to live. No matter how much my mother thought I should. And it wasn't just the miserable weather. I loved the farm and my family. Even if my marriage was over, it didn't mean I had to leave. My life was here. I didn't love the farm just because of Taylor; I loved it because it was a part of me.

I couldn't be in the same room alone with her without feeling the loss, the emptiness. I'd once been proud to call her my wife. Now I referred to her as my business partner. But even that word was used loosely. We had two separate jobs on the farm and these days we rarely overlapped, on purpose.

"Aunty Lorraine," Fran said from the central reception area.

Why was Lorraine here? She was supposed to be with a friend in Queensland. She hadn't told us she was coming home. There were lots of hurried footsteps. I imagined Fran coming around her desk to give Taylor's mum a hug. I walked to my office door.

Fran and Lorraine were holding hands. Lorraine's once brown hair was now grey and short. She didn't care about the grey or her wrinkles. She said it was a privilege to have them because not everyone got older.

"You have no idea," Fran said. Her head whipped to me and then to Taylor, who was standing in her doorway. "I'll go make you a tea." She pushed her glasses up her nose and hurried off to the kitchen.

"Hi, Mum." I walked over to her to give her a hug. She embraced me warmly.

Taylor cocked her head. Could I still call her Mum? I may be split from Taylor, but Lorraine had nurtured me through my adult life. She deserved that title.

"Hi, Mum," Taylor said, making her way to us. "What are you doing here?"

"Isabelle's birthday."

Taylor stared at her.

Lorraine's eyebrows drew together. "You haven't forgotten her birthday, have you? It's bad enough you forget to return my messages."

Taylor scowled. "No." She crossed her arms. "Of course I haven't forgotten."

From the indignation in her voice, I couldn't tell if she'd forgotten or not.

"Isabelle and Callum called me a month ago and begged me to come home for it."

Had they just? Why were they so desperate to have her here? Maybe a month ago, they thought she could have influence over our disintegrated marriage. A lot had happened in a month, though.

I sighed. "We haven't got anything special planned."

Lorraine glanced between Taylor and me. Then she took a step back. And another. Her scrutiny had me shuffling my feet.

"What's going on?" she asked.

"I'm going to help Fran," I said.

Lorraine grabbed my arm. "I don't think so."

I stood still like a child who had disappointed their mother, even though the mother didn't even know it yet.

Taylor's arms were still crossed. "Maybe Isabelle wanted one last get together before Ciaron went back to Ireland."

Lorraine's mouth dropped open. I gritted my teeth. Taylor wouldn't let the idea of me moving go.

"Why would Ciaron be going back to Ireland?"

"Because we're no longer married," Taylor said the words with such derision, I recoiled.

Lorraine's eyes narrowed as she considered us both. "I beg your pardon."

"Ciaron left me."

I grunted. "Yeah. Because it was all my fault. Need I remind you that you checked out a long time ago?"

Lorraine held up her hand. I shut my mouth.

"You're separated? How long?"

"Nearly three months." I gave Taylor a pointed look. Three months and she hadn't told her mother. She had so much disregard for us all. I grimaced. I hadn't told her either, and yet I still thought I could call her Mum.

"Why am I only hearing about this now?" Lorraine asked, anger tinging her words.

Taylor shrugged. She'd been too busy, I suppose. Funny that.

"And you're going back to Ireland?" Lorraine asked me.

Taylor nodded.

"I'm not fucking going back to Ireland." My jaw clenched as I glowered at Taylor. "Stop filling the kids' head with shit. I'm not your father; I'm not leaving my kids or my home."

Lorraine snorted. "Your mother may think differently once she sees you've broken up. She's always had this pipedream that you'll return home."

Just the thought of my mother finding out made me sweat. "I'm not telling her. It's not something she needs to know."

Taylor's arms tightened across her chest. "You're not telling her?"

I exhaled sharply. "This is all new. I want to figure out what my new normal is before I tell her. I don't need her in my ear."

Lorraine's hands went to her hips. "I think she will figure it out herself when she arrives in two days."

"What?" Taylor and I said in unison.

Lorraine grimaced. She couldn't be serious. This could not be happening. My mother was coming here?

I ran my hand down my face. "Are you sure? I didn't think she had a passport or the money for airfare."

Loraine laughed and shook her head. "Those kids probably paid. They offered to pay for me too."

"With what money?" I asked.

"Their savings."

Taylor glanced at me. "Must be the money they were saving for a car."

My brain couldn't form coherent thoughts. My mother

and I had a difficult relationship, which was successful only because I lived overseas and was married to Taylor. Taylor protected me and my sanity. If she was coming here and my relationship with Taylor was in tatters, this visit would not end well.

8

Taylor

I watched as Ciaron's face turned white. I'd read about it in books, but I'd never seen it happen in real life. He paced from one side of the office to the other, pausing, shaking his head and then resuming.

I wanted to go to him and hug him to tell him it would be alright. But I was not that person for him anymore. I remained where I was and watched.

His mother always had this effect on him, even from half a world away. I don't know how many times she'd asked him to help her or one of his siblings. And he did every single time. It was like he was repenting for leaving them.

He stopped pacing, his shoulders sagging, and retreated to his office.

My chest squeezed. His mother always hinted at him going back home one day. Like he would come to his senses or something. Or like he would fall out of love with me, which is exactly what had happened. That was probably why he hadn't told her about our separation. There were many times where I wished he'd stick up for himself. I wanted him to tell her to fuck off because he'd never get the type of love from her that he should. Mum embraced him and gave him that love time and again, something his own mother could never do.

Mum and I stared at his empty doorway.

"Come on, let's go for a drive," Mum said.

Mum and I sat beside each other as we drove around the farm and spoke about the different horses. We stopped outside of Dior's paddock. She would be going back out into a share paddock soon with other dry mares.

"What did the vet find?" Mum asked.

"It was umbilical torsion. The umbilical cord was long, and it twisted around the foetus, cutting off its oxygen."

Mum got out of the car and went to the fence, calling Dior. I followed. Dior trotted over for a pat. I smiled. She must be missing the company of other horses. Usually, she didn't care about humans unless they had food.

Mum stroked her nose. "Ciaron is right. He's not like your father."

"I suppose."

Mum's jaw hardened. "He's always there to support you and the children. Your father wouldn't have helped you with your schoolwork or done half the things Ciaron does."

"Yeah," I murmured. My father had left in my early years of high school. He'd never asked how school was going. He'd barely asked how I was going. And yet I'd let him in my head. Let the memory of him saying to Ciaron that we wouldn't last haunt my thoughts.

Mum continued, "Ciaron helps out around the farm and the house without question."

She didn't need to add 'unlike your father'.

Mum rubbed Dior's cheek. "Why did he move out?"

"That's the million-dollar question."

Mum faced me and raised her eyebrows.

I huffed. "Fine. It's probably the hundred-dollar question."

Mum nodded, urging me to go on.

"He tried to tell me he wasn't happy, and he needed me to be more present, but I didn't listen."

That was the first time I'd admitted it to myself, let alone out loud. There were a million other reasons, but that was the crux of it.

Mum was watching me, expecting more.

"I've been so busy with the farm I didn't have time to listen."

Mum's chest expanded and deflated as if she were reining in her disappointment, because, really, that was no excuse. It was in the hard times that we should have been listening closer to each other.

I scanned the paddocks in front of us. They had been brown for over a year now. I hardly noticed the desolation anymore. The sky changed from a muted blue to grey some days. But not the sort of grey that brought rain. I'd given up on looking for rain clouds on the horizon. Even if it did rain, just once, it wouldn't mean the end of the drought. We'd need normal, consistent rain for that. And then would come the recovery; years of it. "The drought is so draining. What if it lasts another year and we can't keep going?"

"Have you discussed it with Ciaron? Set up an exit strategy?"

I huffed. "No. I cut him off when he wanted to."

There went her expanded chest again. This was going to be a conversation about disappointments, it seemed. "How do you think that made him feel?"

"Like I didn't value him or us."

That must have hurt him. How selfish could one person be? Oh, there was plenty more where that came from. I was the queen of selfish.

"I don't want to lose the farm, Mum. It's been in our family for generations."

Mum nodded. "Farming is tougher now than it ever was. Droughts, floods, mouse plagues, more often and longer. I know you love it here, but it's better to lose the farm than your family." Mum rubbed my arm. "Do you still love him?"

"Yes." There was no doubt in my mind. "But I'm not sure he loves me anymore."

She shook her head. Disappointment. Again. "The pain in his whole being tells me he does. I've never seen a man love someone as much as he loves you."

"I love him that much. And more. I just forgot because it was as natural as breathing."

I missed him and the children so much. I may as well have lived on a different farm for the amount of time I spent with them. What was the point of it all if I didn't have them?

She smiled. "Well, now that you've pulled your head out of your arse, best you fight for him."

"I don't even know where to start. He doesn't even call me his wife. This morning, he called me his partner."

"I'm sure you'll figure it out. He's still wearing his wedding ring. That must mean something."

It was the same problem I'd faced for weeks, months. How to fix something I'd broken that could be beyond repair. It's not like a wound on a horse that could be stitched up. Repairing relationships was much more complicated. Healing hearts, even more so.

By the time we'd finished the tour, I at least knew where to start. When we got back to the office, I left Mum with

Fran and went into Ciaron's office. It was the middle of winter, and yet, my palms were sweaty.

I couldn't let him deal with his mother alone. He'd saved me when we'd first met, and I was in a very similar situation with my father. I needed to do the same for him now. We could fix this. We could fix us. I hope.

I stepped directly in front of him at his desk and waited for him to look up at me. When he did, my stomach was all jittery. I wiped my hands on my jeans. "Your mother will only be here for a couple of weeks." Any longer and I might kill her. "You can move back home, and we can pretend everything is normal."

I was sure we could do it. Before the last few months, we'd been inseparable since the day we'd met, except for the short time when I'd waited for him to arrive in Australia. In that short time, we were connected by our hearts only. After that, we were connected *everywhere*.

"Are you sure?" Ciaron asked, stopping my wandering mind.

"I think it's the best solution, don't you?"

He nodded, his jaw set. Was he about to say something I didn't want to hear? Like it would only be pretend and that's all it could ever be? "Just to make it clear, I have no intention of moving back to Ireland. No matter what." He held eye contact. His voice was strong. I didn't doubt him.

"OK," I whispered, sitting down across from him. My legs couldn't hold me steady any more. All this time I'd been agonising over him leaving because of something my stupid father had said. His firm assurance in this moment was a relief.

"I don't want to put up with her emotional blackmail. On the phone, I can walk away at the end of the call. I can talk to you or the kids." He always had. And at night, in bed, we'd talk about it. I'd comfort him as I wished he'd stop calling her. But he was too good of a person for that.

I reached out, hesitant, my fingers trembling slightly and took his hand. I wanted him to know I was there for him. His rough fingers held onto mine, tethering us together. A small jolt of energy spread up my arm, leaving a slow burn beneath my skin.

"If she doesn't know about the separation, the better for all of us," I said, raising my eyes to his.

He smiled, a sad smile that nearly broke my heart.

"Go and pack," I said. "And while you're at it, think of a suitable punishment for our children."

But while they deserved punishment for their act of deception, I was cheering on the inside because now we had a chance. Or I had a chance to make it right. To earn his love back.

Knowing the kids were on our side, and Mum, would make it so much easier. If Mary ever became aware that we'd fallen out of love, it would be the opening she needed. She'd never been on our side, only on her own. And her own meant getting back at me for taking her son away.

I was betting on being in close quarters with Ciaron magnifying my efforts. Just like those first three days we'd spent together twenty-two years ago, where we declared our love and made a life commitment. I would get that commitment back on track.

9

Ciaron

I called my brother Ronan on the way to the front gate.

"Hello," he said, way too chirpy for 6 am, Irish time.

"Did you forget to tell me something?" I said, not bothering with any preamble.

Silence.

"Maybe that Mam was coming to Australia," I prompted.

"Isn't it grand?" he asked.

If he was standing next to me, I would have punched him.

"No, it's not fucking grand. You know Taylor and I have separated. Now, we are moving back together and pretending to love each other to keep Mam off my back."

He snorted.

"You think this is funny?"

"I didn't tell you because I was sworn to secrecy by my darling niece and nephew. And before you ring the other three, they were sworn to secrecy too."

"What happened to having each other's backs?"

"I'm not exactly sure what the problem is here," he said, ignoring my comment. "I doubt you will have to pretend much. You've loved her since the moment you laid eyes on her."

"What part of separated don't you get?"

"The part where it doesn't fucking make sense."

I groaned.

"Whose idea was it that you move back in?"

"What's that got to do with anything?"

"Answer the question."

"Taylor's."

"As I said, it doesn't make sense." He paused as if he'd just dropped a grenade into the middle of our conversation and was waiting for me to catch up. "I gotta go. The kids will be up soon."

He hung up, and all I could do was stare at the phone and shake my head.

THE SCHOOL BUS pulled up at the wooden front gate as I waited for Isabelle and Callum. They had a lot to answer for. It was bad enough they had *invited* my mother without telling us, but the fact that she was coming, and they hadn't told us, was even worse. People had to prepare for that shit, mentally.

Taylor's support had surprised me. I didn't think she cared anymore. But putting herself in that position to help me showed she did. I'd wanted to kiss her in that moment, from sheer joy and relief.

Living with them as a family and pretending that we were in love would be hard. I would have to remind myself that we were pretending. I could so easily believe it was real.

But it wouldn't be. And that's why I'd need to remind myself it was all make believe. Otherwise, leaving again after two weeks would destroy me.

Isabelle and Callum saw me as soon as they got off the bus and started talking, heads close together as they threw furtive looks my way.

"Hi, Dad," Isabelle said as she approached their farm car.

"Isabelle. Callum. You'd never guess who arrived today."

They shrugged.

"Nanna."

"Really?" Callum asked.

For two conniving little shits, they were good at playing dumb.

"Yeah. And she told some tale about you inviting her to a party that doesn't exist."

Isabelle swallowed. "We didn't say party exactly."

"And imagine our surprise when Nanna said that Mamo will be here in two days."

They threw their bags into the back of their car, ignoring that last revelation.

"And that you paid for her airfare."

Isabelle laughed nervously. "We really wanted to see her."

"Really?"

"Yeah." Callum nodded emphatically. "It's been so long. And we figured it was cheaper for one person to fly than four."

"Uh huh." I was lost for words. "You can follow me back to my place to help me pack."

"Where are you going?" Isabelle's voice was high.

I turned on my heel and went to my car. Let them panic for a few minutes on the drive. It wouldn't be nearly as bad as how I felt when Lorraine said my mother was arriving in two days. My mother, who'd left me to fend for myself for the first time when I was seven.

Mam stood at the front door with a suitcase beside her. A man stood behind her, holding open the door. I didn't know who he was. She bent down. Her face was so close to me it was all I could see. Her lips, covered in dark pink lipstick, stretched into a smile.

"I'm going to go away for a little while with Jim. There is plenty of food in the cupboard for you."

I ducked to the side to look at the big man in the doorway, who must have been Jim, and then back at my mother. "I want to come with you."

"You can't. It's for adults. You need to go to school like a good boy."

I glanced at the man again. He stared right back.

"I can come with you. I'll be good, I promise."

Mam shook her head, her smile disappearing. "No Ciaron, I need a rest."

"Mary," Jim said. His voice was loud and echoed around the entryway.

I shuffled to the side so he couldn't see me and reached out my hand to Mam. Maybe if I could pull her back inside, she would change her mind and stay home with me.

Mam stood up, ignoring my hand. She patted my head. "We'll be home in a few days."

Jim stepped forward and took her suitcase. They turned and went to his car parked a few feet away. Mam never looked back. As they drove away, I ran onto the street and watched as the car disappeared. Then I turned around and walked back inside.

I made myself a sandwich for dinner and watched a movie on TV. Loud voices came from the street. Men were fighting.

They were so close it sounded like they were at the front door. My heart raced faster than I could run, and I could run fast. I tiptoed to the door—every metre seemed like a mile—and made sure it was locked. Then I ran back to my chair and turned the volume up.

I fell asleep while the TV drowned out the night noises.

The next morning, I took myself to school. I came home and did my homework. I started sleeping in my own bed on the second night. But every night before I went upstairs, I would check all the windows were closed and the doors were locked. I left the curtains open in my room so that the streetlights would chase the darkness away.

I ate whatever I could, that didn't require a can opener. I couldn't squeeze it tight enough with my small hands to puncture the can. On day five, I'd run out of food. I took a can of soup to my neighbour and asked them if they could open it for me.

"Where's your mam?" the lady next door asked.

I shrugged.

"Working late, I suppose," she said.

I nodded.

Lying was bad, but not saying words wasn't really lying, was it?

She opened the can for me, and I went back inside and heated the soup in the microwave. I fed myself, washed my clothes, did my homework, cleaned as best as I could for two whole weeks. My best friend at school shared his lunch with me. He told me we couldn't tell anyone because I might be taken away from my mam.

When I got home from school one day, Mamo was in the kitchen sitting at the table. She was looking at me; her gaze going from head to toe and back. Was I in trouble? I didn't want to be in trouble. I didn't want to go to some scary boys' home in the country where they didn't feed you and hit you all the time.

I dropped my bag, and it thumped on the floor. I got ready to run.

Mamo smiled and held her arms out to me. Tears welled in my eyes. I ran into her arms and she smoothed my hair down.

"Where's Mam?" she asked.

I shrugged and nestled into her softness.

"How long has she been gone?"

I shrugged.

"One day?"

I shook my head.

"Two days?"

Another shake.

"A week?"

"No."

"Two weeks."

"A bit more."

"You've been looking after yourself all this time?"

"Yes."

She swore and smoothed down my hair. "Let's pack your suitcase. You can come home with me."

My legs went weak. Her tight embrace saved me from falling.

"Be a good boy and she will come home soon."

Soon meant nearly five weeks later. I was a good boy all those five weeks, because Mamo said if I was good Mam would come home. I must have been bad, and that's why she'd left. I promised myself never to be bad again. I would do whatever I was told. I would help as much as I could. I wouldn't make Mam tired. I tried so hard. But I must have been bad, a lot, because she left four more times after that.

I sighed. No point fretting on something that happened over thirty years ago.

I pulled up in my carport and walked to the house, not waiting for Callum and Isabelle.

Before I even got to the front door, Callum was beside me. His mouth, usually upturned in a smile, was drawn. "Dad, where are you going? Why do you need to pack?"

"I don't want to discuss it right now. Your plan backfired."

Their eyes widened and mouths went slack. As punishment, I think this was working out quite well.

"Dad." Isabelle's voice trembled; she was close to tears.

I swung around to face them, my expression as stern as I could muster. I couldn't keep the charade going though, not when I saw how stricken they were. "I'm moving back in with you while Mamo is here."

Isabelle closed her eyes and Callum let out a hasty breath. Then they shared a look as they tried to hide their smirks.

"I wouldn't be so proud of yourselves. Just because I'm moving back, it doesn't mean your mum and I are getting back together."

Isabelle nodded in that infuriating way her mother does, where she thinks she knows exactly how it will play out, and it's nothing like I think.

"And we'd prefer if Mamo doesn't know about the separation."

"We won't say a word," Isabelle said.

No matter how much you force two people together, you can't make them reconcile, you know, leading a horse to water and all that. Especially if they have given up already. We set to work packing. It didn't take long because I hadn't brought much with me other than clothes. By the time we got home, Taylor and Lorraine were there. The kids hugged their grandmother tightly and Isabelle whispered something in her ear. Lorraine threw a glance my way and nodded.

I shook my head and went to our room. Taylor's room now, but our room again for the next two weeks. Funny how the kids didn't follow. I hated to think that they were together setting more plans in motion. I mean to ask their mamo to visit behind our backs, and pay for her airfare, was something I never thought they were capable of. They could have anything else planned.

I looked around. Nothing had changed since I'd moved out. My space in the wardrobe was empty. Taylor hadn't taken over my spot. I put my clothes away. When I went into the bathroom, it was exactly the same. My side of the vanity was empty. Why had she left it all the same? Did she think I was coming home? Did she want me to?

I wouldn't receive any answers staring at the spaces I'd just filled. I turned to go back out to the living area. I'd probably get no answers out there either. We didn't talk about anything important anymore. We hadn't spoken about our future in a very long time.

Lorraine was standing at the kitchen bench with Callum and Isabelle by her side, chopping onions and zucchini. I smiled, thinking back to when I first moved here and called it a courgette, and everyone thought I was weird.

"Nanna is making us lasagne," Callum said.

"*We* are making lasagne," Lorraine corrected.

I laughed as I sat down at the bench. "Not sure how you roped them in. They usually have the uncanny ability to come out of the woodwork only when the food is ready to be served."

"That's not true," Isabelle said.

Taylor's eyes widened. "What? It's more like five minutes

before it's served because you can't ignore the smell anymore?"

"Yeah. That," Callum said, grinning.

Lorraine considered them. "It's about time you two helped out more. I vote you each cook one meal a week."

"Yes." I almost cheered.

Taylor handed Lorraine a glass of wine before she sat down beside me. "You've just earned that."

This morning, I was living in a separate house and this evening I was back with my family. In a matter of hours, I'd gone from making a breakfast for one in my empty house to watching a meal being prepared for the five of us. It was weird how quickly things could change. But me being here didn't mean anything. Taylor helping me didn't mean anything. It certainly didn't mean we were getting back together and living happily ever after.

"It was nice of Mum to offer you a lifeline," Isabelle said.

Taylor and I glanced at each other. My heart beat quickened.

"Bit like how you saved her that first day you met, huh?" Lorraine said.

Taylor smiled, and it lit up her face like that first day. Giddiness spread through my body almost as strong as it had after our first kiss.

"Tell us again, Dad," Callum said.

"You just want to hear the embarrassing part."

Callum shook his head. "Not just that."

"He wants to hear how you stuck it to Grandpa too," Isabelle said.

Taylor and I glanced at each other again, but this time, I held her gaze as I retold the story. Her chest rose and fell, matching the rhythm of my breath. The air between us was thick, like a fog on a winter morning. "You remember how I first saw her, aye?"

Everyone nodded.

"She was the most beautiful girl I'd ever seen, even when she was sad. Or maybe it was the sadness that made her more beautiful."

Taylor swung her stool around, so our knees were touching. That small connection anchored me to her. No longer a girl, she was the most beautiful woman I'd ever seen. Her brown eyes were so warm and inviting they entrapped me. I stared into them. My heart raced, sending tingles across my skin and numbing my brain. The room faded as I took in her features like I had that first day.

Slowly, it dawned on me that I was supposed to be saying something. "I thought that I would go for it right out of the gate."

Taylor shook her head. "I don't think you thought about it at all."

I shrugged, not hiding my smile. "Maybe."

"Probably. If I wasn't desperate, I would never have been charmed."

"Lucky for me you were."

I stood back as people got out of their kayaks onto the small jetty, with the guide helping. The beautiful girl was next. Her woollen hat was pulled snug over her ears and her brown hair tumbled out from beneath.

I strode forward and held out my hand to her. "I'll help the beautiful cailín.*"*

The guide stepped aside and went to help the next person. The girl took my hand, and my pulse quickened. Her strong grip impressed me. She wasn't fragile. Lucky, I was tethered to her or the lightness in my body might have infiltrated my brain.

"Thank you," she said as her feet hit the wood. Her accent was strange, but one I recognised from my time behind the bar.

"Are you Australian?"

She nodded as she took me in and then stared into my eyes. "Do you work here?"

The tone of her voice implied she knew I didn't. Shit. She figured that out quick.

"No." I held her hand, still, not daring to let her go.

"You just help strangers out of kayaks?"

"Only beautiful ones."

She laughed. "And then what do you do?"

"This." I grinned and leant forward to whisper in her ear. She didn't move away. Warmth radiated between us. "Will you spend the day with me? I'll show you a good time." I rocked back on my heels. My heart was pounding in my chest. Her eyes narrowed. Maybe I should have taken it slower. I didn't normally have to put in the work like this.

She leant forward and whispered in my ear. "You'll need to talk slower, Irish Boy."

I squared my shoulders. OK. Good. I had a chance to fix this. My strong accent had saved me. "Would you like to spend the day with me?"

She smirked. "And you'll show me a good time?"

"Aye." I laughed. "You were playing me?"

"Playing the player? Never." She cocked her head. "How often does preying on innocent tourists work for you?"

"You're my first."

She rolled her brown eyes. "I doubt that."

CALLUM LAUGHED. "You still call Dad, Irish Boy."

She hadn't for a while. Not since the magic had gone out of our relationship. I loved the way she'd said it, like it encompassed everything we were. I longed to hear it again.

"Shush, let Dad finish the story."

I nodded and continued the tale.

THE TOUR GUIDE APPROACHED. *She gave me a once over before saying, "Thank you for joining us, Taylor."*

Taylor. Nice name, bold. I saved it to memory.

She let go of my hand to take the bag the guide was handing to her. "Thank you. No more water activities for me." She glanced at me. "My boyfriend is scared of the water." She grimaced and then lowered her voice as if sharing a dark secret. "Shark bite... right between his legs. Nasty."

The guide's eyes widened while my cheeks went red hot. The guide glanced at my crotch. I closed my stance. Without saying a word, I grabbed Taylor's hand and guided her to the stairs. She threw a wave over her shoulder.

"Shark bite in Dublin?" I asked.

"I'd be more worried about your ability to show me a good time."

She giggled. Her full lips were purple from the cold. She was probably freezing.

I stopped at the top of the stairs, still holding her hand, and turned to face her. Her cheeks were rosy, highlighting her warm brown eyes as she studied me. My eyes drifted to her plump lips. My tongue darted out, licking mine.

"Let me warm you up." I yanked her towards me and covered her lips with mine. She wrapped her arms around my neck as her lips opened. At the first stroke of her tongue, I was a goner. Heat pulsated through me. I held her close, cursing the puffer jacket she was wearing.

What the fuck was wrong with me? Kissing was just kissing.

She pulled away. One side of her lips lifted in a smile. "Thanks. I'm sufficiently warm now."

"I can keep you warm all day."

"No can do, sorry. I've got to head back to my father's farm and the family from hell."

Her sadness was back.

No fucking way was I letting her go that easily. "I'll go with you. I'm good at dealing with hell."

TAYLOR'S EYES were still locked on mine and when her lips lifted in a smile that mirrored hers after our first kiss, heat rushed through me. My breathing faltered. Her cheeks were flushed. Was she reliving the kiss with me? Feeling the connection we had?

The kids laughed about the shark story more than they had when they were younger and made jokes that they were evidence my dick still worked. I'd toned down the kiss. There were some things your children didn't need to hear. They didn't need to hear how I held onto their mum's arse and pulled her close within minutes of meeting her. They didn't need to know the lust that had soared through my body. That I'd thought love at first kiss was absurd, until it wasn't.

"Keep going, Dad," Callum said.

"Not until I have an agreement that you each cook a meal every week." Blackmailing them would work in my favour.

"Fine." Isabelle huffed.

Taylor nudged my knee, and heat radiated from the spot where we touched and landed in my stomach. When I glanced at her, she nodded, encouraging me to add more onto the chores list. I smiled. Good idea to milk this. I'd always wanted them to have a carefree childhood, the total opposite of mine. It had taken a toll as I did more and more around the house. And I wasn't setting them up for life while doing everything for them.

"And you can do the laundry on weekdays," I said, my attention focused on them.

Isabelle and Callum whispered to each other while glancing at Taylor and me. There was a lot of nodding and sly smiles.

Callum stood straight. "We will do the laundry each weekday for this household only."

Taylor nodded. "Agreed."

What the hell? I was getting shafted. After my mother left, I wouldn't be in this household.

Lorraine grinned as she turned to put the lasagne in the oven.

"I think you can tell the rest of the story," I said to Taylor.

She smiled. "It's one of my favourite parts."

It was one of mine too. Because if my kiss hadn't won her over, then this next part certainly won me my wife.

10

Taylor

Mum, the kids and Ciaron looked at me expectantly. What Ciaron had done that night had been simple but effective in winning my heart. I'd never seen anyone stand up to my father like that. Most people were intimidated by his size. That's probably why he hadn't lasted with Mum. She wasn't intimidated by much and he didn't like that.

I made eye contact with Ciaron as we sat opposite each other. His gaze was smouldering, setting my nerve endings on fire. My fingers itched to touch him, to feel the heat of his skin against mine.

Would this moment be as defining for us as the story I was about to tell?

I stared at the ridiculously hot guy standing in front of me offering to go to my father's with me. He was rough around the edges with his five o'clock shadow, rugged hands with a couple of scraped knuckles, tight jeans that hugged his muscular thighs and a tattoo on his arm that poked out the bottom of his jacket sleeve.

I almost laughed, imagining my stepmother's reaction when she saw him. She'd either be swooning or she'd be appalled. Then she'd need to fan herself. It would be worth taking him home for that alone. But even my petty revenge wouldn't extend to taking some random guy home.

"All good," I said, dismissing his offer.

He shook his head. "Showing you a good time extends to chasing your demons away."

I narrowed my eyes at him. "Why?"

"I'm a sucker for a pretty girl who needs help."

"Look, whatever your name is. I don't need some man playing hero. I just need to get through three more days, and I can go back home."

He stuck out his hand. "Ciaron Murphy."

I studied his hand like it might be contaminated. Funny, since I had no qualms about kissing him a minute ago. I shook his hand. "Nice to meet you, Ciaron." I looked around the city. "I'm sure you have plenty of girls falling at your feet. Go help one of them."

He set his jaw. "If I can trump you on the crappy family, will you spend the next three days with me?"

We'd gone from him going to the farm with me to spending three whole days together. Nothing like raising the stakes. What was there to lose? A few more minutes before I caught a train back to hell?

"Fine."

"My father has been in and out of prison since I was two. The only time he is faithful to my mother is when he's in."

I stared at him. Was he telling the truth or making up a story to convince me?

"The only time my mother is faithful is when he's out."

I saw the pain flicker across his face. He wasn't lying. I grabbed his hand and held it tight.

"I'm the oldest child of five. We all have different fathers. Each time she went off with a new man, I had another sibling to take care of."

I didn't have firsthand experience of what he was talking about, but the weight he bore was heavy on my shoulders as if I was a packhorse.

"How old were you the first time she left?"

The wind picked up. My hair whipped around my face. I ignored it, concentrating on him and the way his supple lips formed the words.

"The first time I was seven. By the time I was fifteen, I took her shifts at the bar so we could eat whenever she disappeared. It wasn't legal, but the owner made it work."

My insides were reeling. This man had grown up way faster than he needed to. What sort of mother does that?

"Is she still like that?" I feared the answer.

"She doesn't disappear for months or weeks at a time now. Something happened. I don't know what."

He reached out and pushed my wild hair out of my face. His fingers were gentle as they brushed my cheek. Tingles followed as if my cheek was being kissed by a unicorn.

He'd trumped me on the crap family. I had no choice but to say, "You can spend three days with me."

He grinned, and his green eyes creased at the corners. "I thought you'd never ask."

We walked down the street. The buildings beside us were a mixture of old and modern. The contrast didn't feel out of place; it suited the dynamic vibe of the city. Cars and double-decker busses passed us. The fumes made me miss the clean air of the farm. Their tyres left dry tracks on the otherwise damp road. I knew why it was so green here. Rain was never far away. I hadn't seen a blue sky since I'd arrived.

And people, there were so many people. Dublin was nothing like home. Most of my days were spent on the farm. The only people we saw were our workers.

"Ugh, I never want to live in a city," Isabelle said. "Too many people."

Mum nodded. "They don't even smile and they're always in a rush to get to the next place."

"Where would I ride my bike?" Callum said. "At least here I can just step outside, get on and go for a ride."

I nodded. "These wide-open spaces are perfect for riding our horses."

Was Ciaron going to say something? Tell us about something he liked better here? I held my breath, waiting for him to say something.

"You don't know what you're missing," he said.

My heart dropped. I didn't dare look at the children.

"Pollution, constant noise, drunk people, traffic. It's got a lot going for it."

I breathed a sigh of relief.

"Sounds dreamy," Isabelle said, scrunching up her face.

"More like a nightmare," Ciaron said. "I don't miss it." He nodded to me. "Keep going."

Ciaron held onto my hand like he was never going to let me go.

"Let's get my car and go meet crappy family number two."

"You don't have to do this," I said. "I'm sure I'll be OK."

"If I'm going to marry you, I need to know what I'm getting myself into."

I laughed and kissed him on the cheek. "You're crazy."

But not as crazy as me getting into a car with someone I'd just met. Did serial killer victims feel this safe when they met the person who would take their life? I asked myself this question and yet I still held his hand.

We stopped at an old red Toyota.

"It's not much, but it's mine," Ciaron said.

"As long as we don't break down in the middle of nowhere."

"She hasn't let me down yet. Where are we heading?"

"Killarney."

He started the car, and we headed out of the city. The only reason I knew we were going the right way was because of the few signs I read.

"What sort of farm are we going to, exactly?"

"A horse farm. My father works there."

"OK."

"Do you like horses?"

I pressed my hands together between my legs. His answer meant more to me than it should. Horses were my life. I'd been born into a horse family and so would my future children.

"Haven't met one."

Reasonable, I guess. Most city people hadn't.

"You're in for a treat. They are the best thing on the farm."

Excitement grew in me at the prospect of sharing his first horse experience with him.

"You're not really selling it. It can't be hard to beat your father and crappy family."

I laughed. "Not as crappy as yours, though. My dad left my mum and me when I was twelve. Said he was homesick. I think he was sick of not being put first."

I glanced out the window. Buildings were giving way to more and more green spaces as we left the centre of the city.

"That's why you can understand my Irish accent. Foreigners usually struggle."

I nodded. "A year later, he asked for a divorce because his new girlfriend was pregnant. He was so excited about starting a new family. I don't think he thought how much it hurt me to know I was being replaced."

"Parents can be arseholes."

"I didn't ring him after that. He only called on my birthday and Christmas. Then, out of the blue, he invited me to come and stay for a week."

"And it hasn't gone well?"

"No. The children are feral. I try to ignore them."

"But?"

"Their mother is rude, and my father doesn't say anything."

He grunted. "Been there. It's funny how much my mother's attitude changes every time my father is in jail. When he's out, she loves him and he's the best man in the world. When he's back in, it's the opposite."

I liked his mother less and less every time he spoke about her.

"How do you handle that?"

"It's easier not to say anything, but sometimes I can't hold it in, and I drive the point home that she always goes back to him."

We continued talking the rest of the way to the farm. I told him about my peaceful life in Australia and my mother, who seemed to be the opposite of his. Even after my father had left, she'd kept my life stable, and she managed a successful farm. She didn't hook up with every man who paid her a compliment. She never shirked her responsibility.

When we got to the farm, we were like old friends learning new things about each other.

"You can park over there," I said, pointing to the side of the road opposite my father's house. *We parked and hopped out of the car. Behind the house were lush green paddocks with wooden*

fences. Some of the fences were lined with trees. And dotted around the paddocks were horses.

Ciaron's eyes were wide as he gazed around at the wide-open space.

"What do you think?" I asked as I stood beside him.

"It's like a city park but on steroids." He took a deep breath, like he was savouring the fresh air.

"These are the maiden paddocks," I said.

His eyebrows drew together.

"Maidens are mares who haven't had babies yet." I pointed to a paddock down the road. "That paddock has mares and their foals."

Some mares were lying flat on their side.

"Are they OK? Why are they lying down?" Ciaron asked.

I smiled at the concern in his voice. This man noticed things that many other people would brush off and wasn't afraid to ask questions.

"They're sleeping. Horses can sleep standing up, but to get quality REM sleep, they lie down."

He blushed.

I didn't want him to be embarrassed, so I added, "Usually in the wild, other horses will be keeping watch close by to make sure the sleeping horses are safe."

"None of the others seem to be watching the sleeping ones," he noted.

"No. They all know they're safe here."

Isabelle laughed. "OMG. Dad, you still have a thing for sleeping horses."

She had her elbows resting on the counter and her chin in her hands.

Callum chuckled. "How many times do we have to stop so you can watch a sleeping horse to make sure it's OK?"

"There's nothing wrong with being observant," I remarked. Even though I found his sleeping horse antics amusing.

"If I wasn't observant, I would never have noticed your mother drifting down Liffey River."

"And you two wouldn't exist," Mum said.

"And that would be a tragedy," Ciaron said, smiling at them both.

"A big tragedy," I agreed. "We would have no one to tell this story to."

Not kissing Ciaron would have been a tragedy. Missing out on loving him would be a tragedy. And missing out on sex with him—

"Keep going, Mum," Callum said. He and Isabelle shared a look.

I shifted in my seat. I needed to keep my mind on the task at hand.

Running footsteps approached. *I turned to see Laoise, my eight-year-old half-sister, a red-haired girl with pigtails, running up to us. My seven-year-old half-brother, Sean, was right behind.*

"Who are you?" she asked Ciaron.

I tensed. Did she have to be so rude? OK, maybe I was overreacting. Kids were always curious and forthright with their questions.

"This is my friend Ciaron," I said.

She looked him up and down with a screwed-up mouth, like she had tasted something sour. "Who said you could bring friends to my house?"

I wanted to screw my face up at her. Rude little shit.

"I'm not just Taylor's friend. I'm her boyfriend."

She shot off hollering for our father. Sean followed her lead.

I stared after her, not moving my feet to follow. "That was my sister Laoise. Pleasant, isn't she?"

He rolled his eyes, then took my hand. "Best we go meet my future in laws."

I chuckled and led him towards the house. Dinner would not be boring with him there. And playing the game of being an engaged couple would add some excitement.

"This is going to be a shit storm," I said.

He shrugged. "It depends on them."

My father, a big, burly, brown-haired man, came out of the house. He puffed his chest out as he strode towards us. Orla, his wife, was in his wake, struggling to keep up with him, her face red and patchy. Orla's eyes narrowed at the sight of Ciaron, and her brow furrowed. Their eyes flicked between me and Ciaron and then our hands. My father was much better at hiding his distaste than Laoise was. But his tight lips gave him away.

"Dad, Orla, this is Ciaron Murphy. Ciaron, this is my dad, John and his wife, Orla."

Ciaron stuck his hand out. "Nice to meet you, sir."

Dad shook it gruffly and then addressed me. "Your sister said he's your boyfriend."

I nodded and smiled at Ciaron. He squeezed my hand and gave me a wink. It lit me up from the inside. This man gave me the first bit of comfort and joy I'd felt since I'd arrived in Ireland.

"She wants to take it slow, but she will be my betrothed by the end of the week."

Orla's mouth dropped open. She recovered quickly and snapped it shut. Dad grunted and turned on his heel. So typical. I wanted to roll my eyes, but saw that Orla was studying us closely. Her gaze lingered on Ciaron's jacket and boots and then strayed to his old car. She smirked. I clenched my teeth. Judgemental bitch.

"Come in, Ciaron. Any friend of Taylor's is a friend of ours."

She led the way into the house, her chin high. A shit storm was coming alright.

"Come, sit at the table. I was just about to serve up dinner. Taylor, set a place for Ciaron." Her eyes strayed to Ciaron again. I knew they would. He was just that type of guy; he caught your attention. But the way she cocked her head while studying him was weird.

Dinner started benign enough. The normal get-to-know-you questions.

"Where do you live, Ciaron?" Orla asked.

"Sheriff Street."

"Oh."

"Do you know it?" Ciaron asked.

"Everyone knows Sheriff Street." Her voice was disparaging. She held her hand to her chest. It must have been a rough part of Dublin. I suspect she already knew that by the way she had catalogued everything about him earlier.

I snuck a glance at Ciaron, who was resting against the back of his chair, relaxed. He smiled at me.

"Where do you work?" Orla asked.

She studied his tattoo. I could see it clearly now that his jacket was off, and his sleeves were pushed up his forearm. Reaching from above his wrist was a mixture of Celtic knots, vines and clovers that stretched up and around a Celtic cross that was showcased on his mid-forearm. The cross was like delicate ironwork with a green shamrock at its heart, where an emerald would sit.

"At one of the local pubs, The Shamrock."

Orla nodded, her eyes calculating. "Mmm."

What was she up to? Dad downed a beer and got another one. He didn't offer one to Ciaron.

Laoise piped up. "Do you have horses?"

Ciaron shook his head.

She screwed her nose up. "Why would she want to marry you?"

I took Ciaron's hand. "Because he's nice."

He didn't seem bothered by their questions or their attitude. But I was.

"Oh, I'm sure he is," Orla said. "And strong. You have to be coming from Sheriff Street."

"Dad always said if horses could marry, she'd marry one," Laoise said. "Same as her mam."

Orla smirked. I shifted in my seat.

"Lucky for me, you can't marry horses," Ciaron said. "Looks like she's stuck with me."

"Sounds like you have the Longmire curse," Dad said. He downed half his pint in one gulp.

"The what?" Ciaron asked.

"Your dick is under a spell. Like mine was with her mother. But it will dry up pretty soon and the fantasy will be over."

My potato lodged in my throat. I coughed to loosen it. My face was burning with embarrassment.

Ciaron placed his knife and fork down. "That's not a polite way to speak about Taylor or her mother."

My father shrugged. "Just stating the truth."

"John, not in front of the children," Orla said.

He took another swig of his beer. "We're all fucking friends here, aren't we?" He guffawed raucously. "Ha Ha. Get it. Fucking?" He stared at me. "Didn't take you long. Just like your mother."

I flinched. Bile rose in my throat.

Ciaron stood up and shoved his chair away. "I'd like to say it was nice to meet you, but that would be a lie." He grabbed my hand and pulled me up. *"Taylor, go pack your things."*

I nodded and made my way to the room near the stairs, listening to the conversation behind me.

"You can have her, but mark my words, you'll be back in Ireland soon enough."

I poked my head out the door between throwing things into my suitcase.

Ciaron was glaring at my father. "You know what your problem is? You're a loser. You couldn't stand being with a well-respected, successful woman." He glanced around the table. "So, you had to settle for second best. You can keep your wife and your little brats."

Orla gasped.

Holy shit! My heart raced as I grabbed the rest of my things, still watching as much as I could. I needed to see this family put in their place.

Ciaron turned on Orla. "Don't try to pretend you're better than me." He lifted his lips in a knowing smile. "How many times have you been to the Shamrock Pub?"

She opened her mouth and closed it without uttering a word.

I checked the room one last time before I made my way back to the dining room. I must have set a record for packing, which was probably a good thing, as it was getting tenser by the minute.

Ciaron turned as I approached. Then he gave them all one last look. "Don't expect an invitation to the wedding."

He met me and we walked out hand in hand. We shoved my suitcase in the back and hopped in the car.

I leant over and kissed him. "Thank you."

"I hope this car will start."

"She hasn't failed you yet." I laughed until I cried, probably from relief. We drove into the village.

"How about some dinner and a room for the night?"

"So you can show me a good time?" I joked.
"Anything would have to be better than that."

AT THE CONCLUSION of the story, Mum smiled broadly at Ciaron. "When Taylor told me that story, I knew you were the man for her."

The kids beamed with what I could only describe as pride. In all their lives, they'd only seen their dad angry a handful of times. When he was angry, he meant it.

Like the day we'd argued, and he'd left.

I snuck a look at his tattoo. At his wrist was the traditional Claddagh—two hands embracing a heart adorned with a crown—the symbol of love, loyalty and friendship. He got it in the three days we spent together before I returned to Australia. It matched the ring he gave me, which I still wore on my finger.

Love, loyalty and friendship. As if that man would ever cheat on me. His loyalty and love had never wavered.

I raised my eyes to his. He was watching me. My heart leaped.

We chatted through and after dinner. It was like old times, laughing with Mum and the kids. I missed this—our togetherness. It's amazing what you appreciate after it was gone. Perhaps that was a problem the world over, that people didn't appreciate what they have enough.

Ciaron stood up. "I'm heading to bed. Got an early start tomorrow. Caslicks are coming out."

Mum set her wine glass down. "I'll meet you down at the crush. Seeing I'm here, I may as well help."

He smiled. "You sure are earning your keep. First dinner, then getting the kids to do chores and now farm work."

"Is that elderly abuse?" Callum asked.

Mum's head whipped around. "Who are you calling old?"

Callum shrugged.

Mum stood and put her wine glass in the sink. She shook her head at Callum. "I'll remember this, Callum."

Isabelle laughed. "I'm back to being the favourite."

Callum frowned. "Nanna doesn't have favourites."

Mum squeezed Isabelle's shoulders as she headed for the door. "I'm going home now, Callum. You better think of a way to make this up to me."

He nodded. I could practically see the cogs turning.

We all bid each other goodnight. I followed Ciaron to our room. My hands were sweating again. I imagined him turning on his heel, stalking towards me and kissing me like that first day. I'd wrap my legs around his waist, and he'd push me against the wall, kissing me. His tongue would stroke mine, eliciting a whimper from me as I begged for more.

He didn't.

He continued to our room and stood beside the bed. I made my way around him and grabbed my PJs from where I'd thrown them this morning. I glanced at Ciaron and then at the bathroom. "I'm going to get changed."

For over twenty years, we'd gotten naked and dressed in front of each other. I'd loved sneaking a look at the man who'd won my heart. When did I stop doing that? And why? I didn't find him less attractive. He may have been less toned now, but he still had nice muscles and a nice arse and strong broad shoulders and a big dick. Big.

I shook my head, blushing furiously, even though I was alone. Enough with the dick thoughts. Having sex was not going to fix things. It might not even ease the tension at this rate.

I brushed my teeth, killing time so Ciaron could get changed. The vanity was full again now. His things next to mine, where they belonged. I'd hoped our origin story might reawaken his senses. The way he looked at me suggested it did, but he didn't act on it. I spat my toothpaste out.

When I went back out, Ciaron was sitting on the bed in his PJs. He looked in my direction without making eye contact and then made his way past me. He was so close I could reach out and touch him. I could pull him towards me, if only to feel his touch, his warmth. To remind myself he was here with me. To remind him I still loved him. That our love hadn't dried up.

I didn't. He stepped into the bathroom and shut the door.

When he came back and he hopped into bed, I avoided making eye contact. We were lying so far apart there may as well be an electric fence separating us. But jeez, that fence was powerful. Electric current jumped the gap, sparking across my body.

I let out a nervous laugh, which was more like a bark. "The first night we spent

together was easier than this. At least we knew our boundaries then."

Quietness. Nothing. No response. Was he going to say something?

"You telling me that if I tried anything you would handle me like a 500kg horse probably had something to do with it," he said.

I smiled. "You were so cocky when you whispered 'define anything' into my ear." I spoke to the ceiling instead of turning to him. It felt safer that way, not too personal, even though we were sharing a fond memory and a bed. Even though I wanted to touch him.

He laughed. "And then you 'handled' me so quickly I didn't understand how I landed on the floor."

"But you weren't fazed at all. You got straight back up, wrapped your arm around me and went to sleep."

"It was the best sleep I'd had in years."

I knew now it was because he always slept with one ear open to protect his family. But when he was with me, that pressure disappeared, and he felt serenity. Would he feel that serenity tonight?

I wanted to reach my hand out to his but kept it still against my thigh. Sharing memories could be just that. We couldn't reconnect unless we spoke about our problems. If only we hadn't lost our way. If only I hadn't thought the farm was more important. Do I work backward to address my failures? Would it even make a difference? I had to try. I had to fight. For us.

"Ciaron?"

"Aye."

I stared into the darkness. I wanted to face him, but if he rejected me, I wouldn't be able to hide my pain.

"I'm sorry I accused you of cheating." I inhaled deeply and ploughed on. "I could tell you at least ten reasons why I did it. But nothing excuses it."

In my peripheral vision, Ciaron turned his head to me. He deserved the same from me. I bit my lip before facing him.

"Out of all the things you have done, that has hurt the most."

Tears welled in my eyes. "I know. I'm sorry."

"Can you tell me one of the reasons why?"

"When I saw you so happy and free, I was scared that I'd

lost you forever." My voice trembled. It was at that moment, when I said those hateful words, that I'd lost him completely.

"Thank you for apologising." His voice was flat. He rolled over, his back turned to me.

I let the tears fall silently.

I'd broken his heart and his spirit. I wouldn't blame him if he wanted to go back to Ireland. He said he didn't. And I had to believe that, because our reconciling should not be because of my fear that he might leave. It wasn't, though. I loved Ciaron. My life was empty without him. As empty as his shelves were when he left.

I closed my eyes and imagined Ciaron embracing me like that first night when I'd felt safe and had no concerns about our future. His hands hadn't wandered that night, but I wouldn't stop them now. I wouldn't stop him from doing anything.

11

Ciaron

My senses awakened one by one. Heat spread across my chest and stomach, and a vanilla and honey fragrance filled the air. I opened my eyes. I was spooning Taylor. She wasn't awake yet; she was dead still.

I let her warmth seep into me, and I drew her scent in further so it could infiltrate every part of me. I didn't pull her closer, afraid she might wake. My dick was hard regardless. I imagined exploring her body, my hand gliding over her soft skin, stopping at all the places she liked to be touched, tracing her stretch marks, feeling her nipples harden at my touch. My dick twitched. I sucked in a breath.

It was a guilty pleasure. Guilty because I doubt she'd approve if she knew. How far back in time would I have to go back for this to be normal? How many months? For a long time, holding her like this was the only thing I had left of our relationship, of our love. After our first night together,

I thought I'd be doing this for the rest of my life. Somehow sixty years had been cut down to twenty-two.

I moved away slowly, trying not to wake her, and headed to our ensuite to shower. The hot water helped ease my melancholy and desperate need for her. The water pressure slowed, and the water turned hotter. Someone must have flushed the other toilet. It was too early for the kids. Another sign of an estranged couple; we'd always used the ensuite at the same time before.

I sighed and turned the water off. Enjoying each other's company last night meant nothing in the scheme of things. Maybe our history didn't either. And what about her apology? I had no fucking idea if she was being kind or trying to make amends. Nothing made sense anymore.

I got dressed quickly and went out into the kitchen to make breakfast. I passed Taylor in the hall as she headed back to our room. It was like we were two horses passing through an open gate with blinkers on, not paying attention to the other.

"I've put the jug on," she said.

"Thanks."

I made our coffee and my toast. When I heard the shower turn off, I put bread in the toaster for Taylor and put the jar of Vegemite near her plate. Then I grabbed my keys and headed out for the morning meeting, wondering if Taylor would make an appearance. She didn't. By the time the meeting was over, and I got to the office, the other lady I'd hired for night watch was there waiting.

"Hi, I'm Sofia," she said as I approached.

"Nice to meet you, Sofia. Welcome to Diamond Firetail Farm," I said. "Just let me tell Fran that I'm giving you a tour and we can head off."

We drove around and I pointed out the different buildings, areas and paddocks. She would never remember it all, but it was important to have an understanding of the size of the farm. Sofia was Australian. She'd recently finished an equine TAFE course in Melbourne. She had hands-on experience during her course, and she'd be teamed up with a well-practiced and trusted team member for night watch. Just like Niamh.

Her eyes were wide as she took in all the paddocks. "The farm is bigger than I expected."

"We are small compared to some farms around here, like Woodlands or Coolmore. We're in our second year of drought. Normally it is much greener than this."

I recalled the first time I'd seen the farm here. The grass was lush, often reaching halfway up the horses' legs. It was like the farm in Ireland that Taylor's dad worked at. I couldn't remember seeing anything so green in my life. Now it was brown as far as the eye could see, interspersed with some paddocks that still had grass. Such a contrast.

I stopped the car and pointed to a small grey and white bird on the fence. It had a black band around its neck which continued down the side that was dotted with white spots. "That's a diamond firetail. It gets its name from its bright red rump and upper tail feathers. They mate for life." My heart ached. I'd always thought Taylor and I would last for life. "You'll notice the water troughs have sticks in them. If wildlife falls in, they can climb back out. A lot are desperate for water now with the drought."

Sofia was pleasant and asked a lot of questions about the horses and our processes. I was confident I'd made the right decision with her and Niamh. Taylor wouldn't agree. She hadn't even wanted me to hire them in the first place.

We hadn't spoken about it since the big argument. We hadn't really spoken much. Last night was the most we'd spoken to each other in months. The way she looked at me when we retold our first day reminded me exactly of that day: adoration. Then her apology had come out of nowhere. I shook my head; I needed to stop thinking about it.

When we got back to the carpark, I said, "Well, that's the tour done. You can go to the unit I showed you to unpack your car. Niamh is in the one next door."

She nodded. "Thanks."

"When you're finished, come to the office to fill in your paperwork."

I looked at my watch as she drove away. Lorraine would be waiting for me at the crush. I rushed inside.

"Fran, Sofia is going to unpack and then come in to fill out her paperwork."

"She should have filled it out first," Taylor said.

I swung my head in the direction of her voice. I hadn't seen her standing at Fran's desk. Fran mouthed *sorry*.

"She won't be long," I said.

"Really? What if she gets sidetracked? What if something happens in the meantime?"

I clenched my teeth. I couldn't fucking believe her. She always had to be in control.

"Would you like me to take the paperwork to her now?" My voice was terse.

Taylor shook her head. She opened her mouth and then snapped it shut.

"Fran, let me know if there's a problem and I'll follow it up."

"OK."

I turned on my heel and stormed out.

Fuck me dead. Taylor was right. I should have got all the paperwork signed first. But I'd been too fucking distracted by Taylor, thinking about how we'd woken up and how she'd apologised. The words ran through my head over and over again. Her jealousy and worrying about losing me made no sense. She'd made no attempt to reunite in all the time we'd been apart.

And now her words had me wondering if she wanted to stay married and that had me all kinds of confused. I didn't want to hope for something that was impossible.

I gripped the steering wheel, my knuckles turning white. "She just can't let go, can't let other people make decisions that don't match hers." I shoved my left foot against the footrest so hard my butt lifted off the seat. "She could have texted me to tell me it was a problem. But why do that when she could chew me out in front of someone?"

I arrived at the crush and stared at the steel rectangle box that was like a cage for a horse. The horse would walk in until its chest hit the bar at the front, and the door would close behind it, restricting its movement backwards and forwards. The door was open at the top and enclosed on its bottom half and covered in rubber to protect the horse. The steel bars on either side kept the horse contained, meaning horses and people were kept safe.

The team had brought the horses into the yard, and Rachel and Lorraine were talking. I released muscle by muscle, starting at my toes, and got out of the car. Lorraine broke off as she watched me approach.

"Sorry, I'm late. Are we ready?"

Rachel nodded as she put gloves on. Lorraine grabbed a mare and brought her into the crush. I locked the gate behind her, then handed some Chux and iodine to Rachel. She soaked the cloth and cleaned the mare's vulva.

"I can remember your face the first time we cut open a caslick," Lorraine said.

"Was it the same as when I first saw one put in?"

Lorraine laughed. "I think they were on par. But now you're an expert."

I STOOD beside Taylor as she handed Dan the vet a cloth covered in yellow liquid. A mare who'd recently been covered by a stallion stood in the crush; her foal was in a smaller one right next to her. We were standing behind her.

"Dan is going to wipe down the mare's vulva with iodine. It will clean the area and prevent an infection."

He wiped the cloth dripping in iodine over the area. There was no gentleness involved as he wiped forcefully in all the nooks and crannies. He grabbed a needle off a table. "This is a local which will help."

"Why does she need a local?" I asked.

Taylor had neglected to tell me exactly what a caslick procedure was.

"Are you squeamish, son?"

"It depends on what you're going to do."

"In layman's terms, I'm going to sew up her vulva."

I swallowed. "Yeah, a local sounds like a good idea."

Vet Dan stuck the needle in and injected her in different spots on both sides. My legs tensed. But it seemed she'd barely felt a thing. She only shifted her feet a couple of times. He pinched her vulva and there was no reaction. "We're ready to go."

He grabbed a scalpel. Sunlight reflected off it as he moved it towards the horse. I thought he said he was sewing her up. What did he need a scalpel for? He raised the scalpel and sliced down both sides of the vulva. What the fuck? I clenched my teeth and took a step back. The horse stood perfectly still.

"We cut through the edges of the vulva so we can create fresh skin. This will help when we sew it back together."

I was glad she had sedation. If I was a horse, I'd want all the sedation.

My teeth remained clenched as he got a needle and thread and slowly sewed the edges back together.

Dan glanced at me and chuckled. "Good to see you're still with us."

"This is worse than seeing someone glassed in a bar fight."

There were so many intricacies to this horse breeding business I wondered if I'd ever be able to know them all. I'd need to learn them, even if they creeped me out. This farm was Taylor's life and, by extension, it was now a part of mine. I would never have thought our meeting a few months ago would lead me to being so intimate with a horse's reproductive system.

Dan turned back to his sewing task. "This horse has poor anatomy. The vulva doesn't seal properly, which means the uterus is not protected. Sewing the vulva like this will prevent endometritis and placentitis."

"What's that?" I asked.

"It's a bacterial or fungus infection that affects the placenta. Not good. It causes premature delivery and pregnancy loss."

"This simple procedure can be lifesaving for mare and foal," Taylor said.

When Dan finished sewing, I let out a long breath. Taylor opened the front gate, and the mare walked away with her foal following like nothing had happened.

Taylor smiled at me. "You did good, Irish Boy."

I wanted to thrust my chest out and beat on it with my fists.

"One caslick down, a million more in your lifetime to go," Dan said.

A million more. I was ready for them all.

Dan put the needle and thread down, and the vet nurse cleaned the table ready for the next horse. "In a few months' time, when she is close to birthing, we will remove the caslick."

. . .

Even though Mum thought I was a pro, I'd still cringe from time to time. There was so much to horse breeding the public didn't know. I'd learnt every last thing that I could about this farm and horse breeding. It was a part of me now.

Rachel gave the mare an injection of local into her vulva and then tested the site to see if it was numb enough. She slid two fingers up behind the stitched skin and spread them into a V to stretch out the skin of the vulva. Then she cut along the whole length of the stitched skin. The removal of the caslick would mean an easier birth for the mare and foal. The danger period for infection was over.

Lorraine and Rachel chatted as they swapped one horse for another and removed their caslicks. I was on autopilot as I handed equipment to Rachel.

I tensed as I thought back to earlier and how Taylor once again tried to enforce her dominance and put me down in front of others. Her apology last night was just that, an apology. She wasn't trying to set a beginning for our future. I should never have let myself fall into that daydream.

"Ciaron," Lorraine said.

I glanced at her. Rachel had moved away.

"We're done."

"OK."

She studied me. "What's going on? You've hardly said a word all morning."

I searched for Rachel. She was talking to a stud hand by the fence and wasn't in earshot.

Lorraine moved closer to me, drawing my attention to her, before saying, "Last night was nice. We had fun. We laughed. Did something happen this morning?"

I sighed. "It was the same old Taylor this morning." I looked down at my feet and kicked the dirt. "She told me off in front of Fran."

"What about?" she said gently.

"I didn't get the new worker to sign all her forms before she moved in."

Lorraine tightened her lips. "You know that you should have."

I didn't acknowledge her reprimand. "She didn't have to chew me out in front of Fran."

"Ciaron." Her voice was stern.

I swallowed. "Yes, Sofia should have signed her paperwork first."

"Because the one time Taylor didn't get it signed first, she then forgot altogether, and we couldn't withhold wages when a house was damaged."

I nodded. It had cost us thousands and Taylor had never forgiven herself. We had all made sure not to make the same mistake again.

"Maybe she shouldn't have done it in front of Fran, but she probably thought it was just Fran."

"Maybe." Lorraine was right. Fran was always there. She heard everything.

"What made you forget to get the forms signed? That's not like you."

I looked away. "I was distracted."

"About?"

Did I really want to tell her? Admit that I was weak and was hoping for something impossible? This was Lorraine. If anything, she'd help me with my feelings.

"Taylor," I said.

"What about Taylor?"

How much had Taylor told her? What had the kids said?

I'd tried to keep a lot from them. I didn't want them exposed to how I was feeling. I didn't want to influence their feelings for Taylor or myself.

"I don't know."

I looked around and saw that Rachel had left us. I relaxed my shoulders, ready to speak freely.

"Let's go for a walk," Lorraine said.

That was a good idea. Less opportunity for me to gather nervous energy.

"What about Taylor had you distracted?"

"Last night was nice. It reminded me of old times, when we were happy."

Lorraine nodded and smiled. "You have to hand it to those kids; they set the night up perfectly. They knew exactly how much you both like to share that story."

She was right. Bloody kids. They'd bided their time, waited until our defences were down, and then, wham, asked us to recite our story. Did they really think one retelling could fix all our problems? Maybe not. Maybe the whole point was to get us talking. My head hurt thinking about what else they might have planned.

We walked along the road, paddocks lined both sides. Without rain, the road had become dusty. With every footstep, a small plume of dust rose around our feet. The horses were dusty. We were dusty. Our homes were dusty. The windows weren't clear glass anymore. Sometimes we'd wash them with the water from the washing machine. It wasn't exactly clean water, but using it with the sponge and squeegee was effective.

The grass was more brown than green in the paddocks around us. Because the maidens living there weren't pregnant, they didn't need as much extra feed yet. Even the leaves on the trees were brown and fragile. It's like we were all losing our colour.

"Remembering the happy times isn't a good thing?" Lorraine asked, breaking the silence.

"I enjoyed it too much. But I can't live in the past. Too much has happened since then."

"Tell me about that. Taylor hasn't said much."

It didn't surprise me. I was the talker in the family these days.

"She's been so focused on the farm she has practically forgotten we exist." I let out a breath. I'd thought about this so many times, and yet it was hard to release those thoughts. "There were so many things. Isabelle fell behind at school and was struggling. Her friend choices weren't great."

"What about Callum?"

"Callum was Callum—chill. I felt so bad that he wasn't getting as much from me as Isabelle. And then I found him growing a couple of marijuana plants in the top paddock."

"Oh. A bit too chill then." She chuckled. And now, I could see the humour. Not so much back then, though.

"Oh, alright. He thought it would be good for him and Isabelle. They'd been smoking for a few weeks before I found out."

"How did you find out?"

"The smell gave them away when they made weed brownies."

She laughed.

"Lucky they just kept it to themselves."

"Their friends probably had their own plants. Callum must have got the seeds from somewhere."

"Yeah. I had that conversation with their friends' parents. That was fun."

"*You* had the conversation with them? Alone?"

I shrugged. There was so much to say, but it boiled down to one thing. "Taylor didn't care. It was all left up to me."

I stopped walking and went to a fence, resting my forearms on it, looking towards the river. The river was shallower now, and it had shrunk away from the riverbanks. We were lucky there was water still in it. Some rivers had dried up altogether.

One town close by had run out of water completely and the council had to truck water in every day until they could build a pipeline. And there were reports of many other towns in the same situation.

Lorraine glanced at me. "But that wasn't the only reason you broke up, was it?"

"No. We stopped talking. She made decisions about the farm without discussing it with me. She was angry all the time. Even the kids felt it. I thought it was the stress from the drought, so I didn't say anything."

I kicked at the dirt below the fence. Dirt where once grass would have been. When the drought was over, how long would it take for me to get sick of spraying the fence line?

Lorraine was silent beside me, waiting for more.

"On top of that, she'd question me and my decisions in front of the team, putting me down and making me feel incapable." I let out a huff. "*I* didn't matter anymore."

The truth hurt as much today as the first time I thought it. All my life, until I'd met Taylor, my needs didn't matter. My mother only thought of herself, and that meant I had four brothers to think of. What I wanted or needed was irrelevant. Months ago, that feeling had creeped in again until it settled, like the dust around us had settled.

No point stopping there. Time for the killer blow. "Then

at parent-teacher interviews, she accused me of cheating. We'd broken up by then, but the accusation..."

Lorraine swung her head to face me, the whites of her eyes increasing with every centimetre.

I met her eyes.

"Taylor accused you of cheating?"

I nodded.

She rubbed my arm. "That must have hurt."

"She apologised last night. I wanted to believe she was truly sorry. But I don't know. It's hard to believe after everything else."

"I don't think Taylor would apologise if she didn't mean it."

I rubbed my eyes. "I suppose."

"Do you want to save your marriage?"

I stared out into the distance. Did I? I'd tried for so long I didn't know if it was possible anymore. But I'd felt hope last night. So that must mean something. Either that or I was a fool for believing in love.

"Yes. But I don't know how. I don't know what else I can do."

"You can start by trusting her. You can trust how genuine she is."

That was true. Her feelings were generally open. What had she said last night about why she'd accused me of cheating? It was because she was scared. Feelings I needed to take into consideration. Fear could make us irrational. Just as irrational as love.

Lorraine rested her hand on my arm. "You're not blame free here, Ciaron. I want you to think about that."

I closed my eyes. If I wanted this to work, I needed to change too. But I had no idea in what way. Whatever it was, I needed to figure it out.

12

Taylor

Mum, Ciaron and I were in the kitchen doing the dishes after dinner. The kids had taken themselves off to their rooms. A deliberate act to avoid work? Perhaps. Maybe it was a good idea. Dinner hadn't been full of fun reminiscing, like it had been the night before. Ciaron had gone from being light and happy to sullen and back again. He'd been hard to read, and I couldn't put a finger on why.

"Fran tells me that Sophia filled her forms in," Mum said. "So, crisis averted."

Ciaron stiffened.

I shoved the tea towel into the glass. "How did you know about that?"

"Ciaron was upset when he got down to the crush. He told me about what happened."

I yanked the tea towel out and thrust the glass at Mum, ignoring Ciaron, who was washing dishes beside me. I couldn't believe he went to Mum like he was a child tattling on a sibling. I'd done nothing wrong. It's not my fault he got *upset* when I pointed out his error.

I raised my eyebrows at Mum. "And why was he so upset? Because he made a mistake?"

Mum opened her mouth, but she was cut off by Ciaron's angry voice. "Because you've never made a mistake?"

I wrung the tea towel in my hands. Time to turn it around on Taylor, is it? Fuck that. I wasn't always to blame. "It's not that hard a concept. They fill in the forms before they move in."

"So what, now you're going to have a fucking go at me in front of Mum? Because doing it in front of Fran wasn't enough?"

I rounded on him. "I'm not the one who told Mum all about it."

Ciaron's face was flushed. "She saw that I was upset and had the decency to ask me about it. Unlike you."

"You were upset because you didn't follow the process."

Mum stepped forward. "Ciaron, you should have told Taylor you were upset by her actions."

Ciaron's narrowed eyes didn't waver as he stared at me. "I've told her before, but she didn't listen. She never fucking listens."

That was bullshit. He never told me that. I was so sick of being cast as the villain. He was always the good guy. The kids thought he was. Mum thought he was. He hadn't told me anything of the sort. It's not like we'd spoken since the argument. The argument...oh wait...the day he decided to leave me and the kids, he'd mentioned it then. I'd been too busy thinking about the *I've had enough* part.

"Taylor, has Ciaron spoken to you about this before?"

"I wouldn't call it speaking to me. He yelled it at me."

"Because you never fucking listen."

Mum held her hands up. I took a step back.

He did something wrong. I called him out on it. They were facts. But life wasn't just about facts, it was about feelings, too. I chewed on my lip.

Mum stood directly in front of us. "You are not going to repair your relationship if you can't talk or listen to each other."

I needed to pull my head in. "I should have thought about how I spoke to you about it this morning."

Ciaron didn't say a word, didn't give an inch. That was so unlike him. He was usually the peacemaker. Had I really pushed him this far? Was there no hope? I had to believe there was. Last night I thought we'd made some inroads. But Mum was right. If we didn't speak about our problems and find a way to fix them, there wouldn't be much hope.

"Ciaron?" Mum asked.

He stared a while longer. My heart rate increased. Please say something. Please.

"I should have admitted I'd made a mistake." He rubbed the back of his neck. "And I should have told Taylor I had a problem with the way she spoke this morning."

Mum rested her hand on each of our shoulders. "You can do this. I know you can. Please be patient with each other and listen."

I nodded. Ciaron turned back to the sink and resumed washing. I dried the next glass. And Mum put the last one away. This was the first step in many. I needed to remember we hadn't got here overnight, and we wouldn't be out of it overnight. We'd need to try to talk like two rational and mature people without letting the anger and resentment get in the way.

It wasn't going to be easy. Yes, we'd made mistakes today, but we were still both here, not giving up.

We could do this.

13

Ciaron

When Lorraine left, I followed Taylor to our room. One night later and it still felt weird. Normally, we'd brush past each other as we got ready for bed. Now we stood in the doorway staring into the space.

"Do you want to shower in here?" I asked. "I can go to the other bathroom."

"OK. Thanks."

I moved past her. "Just let me grab my toothbrush."

I went into the ensuite. When I came out, Taylor was standing just outside with her PJs in hand. She gave me a small smile as I walked past. This was so bloody awkward. It's like we were two strangers living in the same house.

I hopped into the shower and turned the hourglass timer I'd put in there for the kids. We were in drought and twenty-minute showers were not acceptable.

I needed to start considering how Taylor was feeling in our darkest days too. I know I felt lonely, but she probably did as well. And isolated. Why the hell couldn't she have just listened when I'd tried to speak to her? Maybe even worked less and helped me with the kids? It was like I was a single parent before I was even a single parent.

I rested my hand against the wall as the water spilled down my back. Taylor was in the shower a few rooms away, naked, water cascading over her curves. I knew what every one of them looked like. What they felt like. We'd showered many times together, touching, tasting, fucking. My fingers twitched, remembering what they felt like. Fuck. I wanted her in every way possible.

My other hand wrapped around my dick. Images of me taking her flicked through my mind. Us on top of a haystack. In the river. Her riding me in the office. In the barn. More and more. I paused on our first time. The morning after we met.

Taylor snuggled up closer to me as the morning sun filtered in the hotel window. So close, there was no space between us, from our shoulders to our ankles. My lips brushed her neck. She sighed in response.

"Good morning," I said.

She pushed her butt against my hardness. "Seems like you're ready to show me a good time."

A jolt of energy pulsated through me. "Are you ready?"

"Show me what you got, Irish Boy."

I reached my hand up and brushed her hair away before suckling on her neck. I ran my hand down her side, her waist, her hip, and found the hem of her sleep top. My fingers tingled, almost shook, as they touched her bare skin. I found her breast and squeezed. Her breath faltered ever so slightly. I pinched her hard nipple and was rewarded with a small moan.

I paid the same attention to her other breast. Her back arched, pushing her butt into my hard-on again. I nibbled on her earlobe as my hand skimmed the skin of her stomach before reaching into her pants and underwear. Taylor opened her legs as my fingers travelled through her wetness.

My hand was restricted by her underwear. Fuck it. I pulled my hand out and grabbed her PJs and undies and tugged them down. Taylor rolled onto her back and kicked them off.

"Take your top off," I demanded.

She did.

I pulled the bedcovers down so I could see her naked before me. Her legs and arms were tanned and her torso a milky cream. There was a small round birthmark on her hip. Her breasts fell slightly to the sides. Holy fuck. I wanted to touch her everywhere, kiss her everywhere.

I tore my t-shirt off and my underwear wasn't far behind. She raked her eyes across my body and wet her lips. My heart thumped in my chest as we stared at each other.

I was supposed to be showing her a good time instead of getting my rocks off just staring at her. My hand returned to her slick folds. I lowered my lips to hers and swept my tongue across the seam. Her lips parted and invited me in. Our tongues met stroke for stroke, and my fingers matched the movement.

I pushed her legs open with my hand and she opened them wider. I slipped two fingers in and pumped. Our mouths disengaged as she let out a moan. I slid my fingers out and found her clit. She was so fucking wet. I circled her clit and rubbed it, all the while watching her face to see what she liked best. When I figured out exactly what she wanted, my fingers were relentless as I drove her to the edge.

She bent her legs up and forced her feet into the mattress. It dipped slightly at my knees. Taylor's breaths were haggard.

"I'm going to make you come so fucking hard the whole bed will shake."

Taylor threw her head back and cried out. My fingers slowed, coaxing her.

"Come for me, Taylor. Come all over my hand."

Her legs shook.

"Later it will be in my mouth. I want to taste you so bad."

She cried out my name as her whole body shuddered. I slowed my fingers more and her tremors matched the movements. The bed shook beneath us.

Good time, achieved.

As her breathing returned to normal, I scrambled for a condom. I needed to be inside her so bad. I needed to feel her warm tightness around my dick. I rolled it on as fast as I could and moved in between her legs. I gazed into her eyes to make sure she was ready. A small smile lifted her lips.

I pushed in centimetre by centimetre. She tensed beneath me and her mouth opened into an O. But she didn't tell me to stop. I pushed myself all the way in and out, lubricating my length.

Taylor shifted below me, changing position and bending her legs so she could take me deeper. With every stroke a ball of tension built inside me.

"Harder," she said.

I thrust. The tension built. I adjusted my hips. Taylor let out a small whimper.

I pulled back a little.

"Don't stop," she begged. She gripped my shoulders. I drove into her. She squeezed her pussy around my dick and held the pressure.

"Holy fuck," I grunted.

Taylor cried out. Her hold on my shoulders tightened. My whole body shuddered as my balls clenched and released. The tension let go in a burst and I exploded inside her. There was no more pumping as a growl escaped from my throat.

Our chests heaved against each other as I stared down at her. The hair at her temples was wet and her face was flushed. My whole body was flushed.

"That was the best fucking sex I've ever had," I said.

Taylor nodded and smiled. "You lived up to your promise to show me a good time."

"That promise is for the rest of our lives."

My hand stilled as I exploded in it, thinking about her loud cry. I grunted as I emptied myself out. I stood straight and let the water cleanse me before turning the shower off. The timer filtered its last grains of sand into the bottom glass as I glanced at it. Ha. Good timing.

As I dried myself, I realised my mistake. Pleasuring myself with my hand wasn't it. The fact that I'd left my PJs in our bedroom was. Now I'd have to go back there in nothing but a towel and get dressed in front of Taylor. Even as I walked down the hallway, and the cold air prickled my skin I felt nothing but heat rush through my body. This was ridiculous. We were still married, being naked in front of each other was natural. Except now it was anything but.

I opened the door and scanned the room. Taylor was in bed, looking at her phone. I traipsed to the bed, letting the towel drop when I got there. How would she react to my brazenness? Taylor stiffened and her eyes widened, but she didn't move her head or eyes in my direction. She didn't move them away either. I don't know if I could have been that nonchalant if she was naked near me.

I got dressed into my PJs and slid into bed beside her. Her warmth radiated towards me. She was so close but untouchable. Memories of our first time together flooded my mind, and my whole body ached with want, with need. I wished I could hold her like I had afterwards. If I hadn't already been in love with her before we'd had sex, I certainly was after.

Would sex even kill the tension between us? My fingers twitched, wanting to reach for her, to touch her, feel her succumb to that touch. Every inch between us felt like another mile in a horse race. The finish post stretching further away even though it was within reach.

Taylor put her phone away and turned off the lamp. "Goodnight, Ciaron."

I swallowed the lump in my throat. "Goodnight."

And there went another night without any intimacy. We weren't ready for that. My brain understood, but my heart wanted it so bad. My skin craved her touch. But we still had issues to work through, and we had to prove ourselves to each other. It wouldn't be as easy as facing her father this time.

I lay on my back and closed my eyes, listening to her soft breathing. I'd promised the rest of our lives. And I still wanted it. Time to work a little harder on forgiveness and acceptance and loving the shit out of her. And figuring out my part in this mess.

14

Taylor

Mum pulled into the carpark at the office with Mary in the passenger seat. Show time. I stood and walked out into the reception area. Ciaron came out of his office and stood beside me. I gave his hand a squeeze.

I heard Mary and her strong Irish accent before she even entered the building. Taking a deep breath, I plastered a smile on my face. I would be pleasant, like always, but there was no way she was stealing my husband away or creating a rift bigger than we ourselves had caused. I held on tight to Ciaron's hand.

Mum led the way into the office and moved to the side for Mary. She'd aged since we'd last seen her in person years ago. The lines on her face were deeper and her frown more prominent. Was her heavy makeup an attempt to cover them up? Was her bright lipstick an attempt to draw our attention away from the lines around her mouth? Her lips were fuller than I remembered. Lip filler maybe? Her light brown hair dye with blonde highlights, was probably an attempt to look more youthful. It covered her grey perfectly.

Mum and I looked plain in comparison.

As soon as she spotted Ciaron, a smile erupted on her face. She made a beeline for him. He met her halfway and was nearly knocked over by her energy. She saved him by wrapping her arms around him.

If it was anyone else, I would have relished the joy. But I'd always struggled with Mary. I really needed to let it go. Ciaron didn't let his past bother him and neither should I. Maybe it was because she was always trying to undermine our relationship, or maybe I was jealous, but that didn't make sense because he'd chosen me over her.

She stepped away and cupped his cheek. "You look tired."

"It's been a long year."

The drought and our separation had taken its toll on him. Meaning I had taken my toll on him.

"We are only halfway through," she said.

I stepped forward to save Ciaron from receiving the third degree. "Hi, Mary."

She pulled me into a hug. "Taylor."

"How was your flight?" I asked as she let me go.

"Good. Good. Long."

"You must be tired. How about we have an early lunch and then you can rest and settle in before the kids get home?"

"Aye."

"You'll be staying with Mum."

Mary's eyes narrowed, she glanced at Ciaron.

Maybe I should have lessened the blow instead of throwing it out there.

"She has more room than us," I said. "She lives here on the farm. It's only a five-minute walk from our house."

A frown settled on her face. Ciaron shifted beside me. Shit. I'd overstepped the mark again. Mum had told me I needed to stop doing this. I should have spoken to Ciaron about it first.

Ciaron nodded. "It will be much better than staying with us. We get up early for work."

Mary's frown deepened. "You're going to work while I'm here?"

My stomach tightened. She was disappointed, and Ciaron and the children would be too. We'd need to figure something out. We should have discussed it days ago but I'd never thought about it. That was selfish of me.

"Not all the time," Ciaron said. "But breeding season is the busiest time of year for us. There are some days we can't avoid work."

Mum stepped forward and rested her hand on Mary's arm. "I'll bring you to the afternoon meeting. Then you will see what Ciaron means."

Ciaran nodded. "Great idea. We'll meet you at your place for lunch in a few minutes."

We watched them walk out, and then I followed Ciaron into his office. I needed to own what I'd done.

"I'm sorry I didn't discuss where your mum was going to stay. If you want her to stay with us, I can say we changed our mind."

Ciaron shook his head. "I think the separation is good." He gave me a wistful smile. "I've become closer to Mam since moving here. I've gained perspective on how broken she was. You helped with that."

I didn't dare tell him that I thought she still was. I could be overreacting, but I didn't think so. I think she was still the horrible person she always was but could hide it better thousands of kilometres away.

He came and stood in front of me. "I'm scared if I get too close...I don't know...maybe...I'll realise she chose to be that way because she doesn't love me."

The breath was sucked out of me. I reached out and took his hands, thoughts slamming into every corner of my brain. I needed to show him that he was loved. I needed him to see that he was valued. I needed him to know that his worth was not dependent on her. My every thought focused on mending his heart. The one I'd broken.

"I love you, Ciaron. I choose to be a different person. I promise I will try to be the wife you deserve."

They were big words. I knew that. I needed him to believe they were as true as my heart knew them to be. Nothing mattered more than that, not my pride, not my fear.

And I would...I would try my hardest. And I would prove it...as long as Mary didn't interfere. As long as we had the space to heal, and she didn't infect us with her poison.

I waited for his reaction. Everything inside me begged for him to believe me.

He pulled me closer, his eyes locked on mine. "Thank you." He kissed me gently and my lips tingled. "Not just for your promise, but for your support as well."

My heart lifted. I knew they were only words we'd shared, but they were the most heartfelt words we'd said to each other in a long time. We had always been stronger together and now it was time to prove we still were.

And...he kissed me! He freaking kissed me. Those gentle lips were on mine for a mere moment, and I wanted to cheer for the whole world to hear.

CIARON STOOD at the front of the meeting room, remote control in hand. He commanded the room, by presence alone, as a good leader should. Everyone on the farm, whether they were horse staff or not, sat at the tables and faced him. Mary and Mum sat beside me at the back of the room.

"Thanks everyone for coming. We're going to watch a short video now. For those of you who don't deal with the horses day to day, or haven't been involved in breeding, this will show you signs to look out for. For everyone else, this is a refresher. If you think you see something like this or if a horse is acting strange, put a call over the two-way and one of the horse staff will attend."

I leant towards Mary. "The video was Ciaron's idea. Over the years it's saved many lives."

Mum nodded. "We can tell staff what to expect but showing them like this is even better."

We watched the start of the video which showed us how to tell if a horse was getting close to foaling.

"OK," Ciaron said. "Can someone tell me one of the signs?"

"Bagging up," someone called out.

"Right, the udder becomes larger," Ciaron said. "Anyone else?"

"Waxing up, the teats look waxy."

"Aye."

"The vulva loosens."

"Aye. The last common one now. Think of a human."

"The shape of her belly changes as the foal drops."

"Perfect."

Ciaron looked around the room. "We don't expect the non-horse staff to recognise all of this. But horse staff will be looking for these signs every day. You may think that this makes it easy. Not necessarily. Some horses don't show any signs until they're in labour, others might only show one or two."

He repeated the signs again. And added a few more, including different behaviours. I enjoyed watching him and the way he moved and made eye contact with everyone. The passion in his voice fuelled their enthusiasm. And his smile; it lifted everyone up.

Over the years some of the new short-term staff would be enraptured by him, and even blush if he looked their way, but he never took any notice. And they soon got over it. Observing him, I could see why his charisma would have that effect. *And* his body. He had a damn fine arse and muscular legs. I must have forgotten to pay attention over the years. Stupid me. I loved Ciaron but forgot to be in love with him.

Maybe that's what happened when you were married for a long time. Your love changed to a *content* type of love instead of a *need you* type of love. The drought would have contributed too. The longer hours and more hands on we became the more tired we were. We existed beside each other but not in each other.

"OK, what about when a horse is in labour," Ciaron said, drawing my attention back to the meeting. "What do we expect to see?"

Everyone discussed it at length and then Ciaron continued the video. I watched him as he leant against a table at the front of the room. The angle he was on caused his green work shirt to stretch across his broad shoulders and chest. His hands rested on the edge of the table. Those calloused but gentle hands could work wonders on my body.

Ciaron looked at me almost as if he knew I was checking

him out. I didn't avert my eyes. His mouth lifted on one side. My heart leapt. There was a glimmer in his eyes I hadn't seen in a long time. I returned his smile.

"OK. Now that we've all watched the video, Ciaron's next question will be what are the signs of labour, what did we miss before," Rachel said.

Ciaron broke eye contact and stood up. The video had finished, and we hadn't even noticed. I glanced at Rachel who was smirking at me. I blushed as I tried not to grin at her and turned my attention back to the discussion.

After that segment came difficult labours. With every new segment, Mary's eyes widened. When the video showed chains being used to pull a foal out, her hands clenched.

The video stopped. Ciaron addressed us all again. "This is the best time of year on the farm. Watching a new life come into this world and being a part of it is exhilarating. It can also be heartbreaking. We can do everything right but still lose a mare or foal."

Nods from the staff.

"I want you to remember we are all a team. If something doesn't feel right, make the call. You won't be the first person to think a horse was in labour when all it was doing was having a snooze."

Rachel laughed and called out, "How many times has that happened to you, Ciaron?"

He cracked a grin. "I don't know Rachel. Are you keeping count?"

I loved how he could lighten the mood in a room by making fun of himself, that he wasn't embarrassed about his mistakes.

"I think it was three times last year," he said.

"That we know about. How many was it, Taylor?" Rachel said.

All eyes turned to me. How did she know that Ciaron and I were no longer in silent mode and we could now tease each other again? News travelled fast on the farm.

I chuckled. "I don't think it's fair to betray my dear husband's confidence."

Rachel rolled her eyes.

I grinned at Ciaron. His eyes widened when he realised what was coming.

"I can say it was at least six," I said.

Rachel roared with laughter.

Ciaron shook his head at me even while he smiled. My grin widened. It had been a long time since we could poke fun at each other.

"That concludes our meeting," Ciaron said. "Thanks for your time. My wife will not be sharing any more secrets today."

Wife—my heart raced at that word. He'd called me his wife.

"There's always tomorrow," Rachel said, giving me a high five before making her way out the door.

"I never knew so much could go wrong," Mary said.

"That's why Ciaron and I need to work during breeding season," I said. "Some of these horses are worth hundreds of thousands of dollars. We are the most experienced people on staff."

Ciaron had come to stand beside us. He rested his hand on the back of my neck sending tingles through me. I leant towards him so I could have more contact.

"Not only that," Ciaron said, "but this is our business. We are ultimately responsible for every life on this farm,"

We were ultimately responsible. We. It appeared I'd been the only one to forget that.

15

Ciaron

I turned off my computer and stood up. The kids would be home soon, and I was looking forward to spending time with them and Mam. Taylor came into my office and sat in one of the chairs. Her palms lay flat on top of her thighs. What was she about to tell me? I clenched my jaw and sat back down.

"I was thinking." Taylor paused and looked at the ceiling before returning her gaze to me.

Whatever she was thinking must have been hard for her. My shoulders tensed as I waited.

"Maybe we don't need to be on call every night this season. Maybe we can share with Rachel. It's time she had more responsibility. She has earned it and I trust her. Being on call and call outs during the season are part of her management contract. We should start utilising it." It all came rushing out like she wanted to say it before she could take it back.

I opened my mouth.

"I know it sort of goes against what I said to your mam about us needing to be here. But, we will still be here; we live here. Rachel can call us if she needs to. But we don't need to be first people the night watch call. We can do week on/week off with her." She stopped talking and stared at me, her brown eyes wide. Had she really said that? All of that? I waited to make sure she was finished.

"You've never wanted to relinquish control before," I said.

"I know," she said quietly.

"So what's changed?"

"A lot. Everything. I don't want to lose you, Ciaron."

I took a deep breath in. Was that the only reason? It was a good one from my selfish point of view, but fear wasn't a sustainable reason.

I shifted in my seat. "OK"

"We can't continue this way, Ciaron. Not you, me or the kids. I miss so much time with you all, I may as well not even be part of the family." She sighed. "Like Callum. He hasn't been riding lately. This morning I noticed his bike sitting near the shed."

"It's broken. Vet Dan said he will try to help me fix it. His son is a bike mechanic."

"I should know these things," she said.

These were the words I'd wanted to hear for so long. But could she actually do it? Change her whole way of being?

"Rachel has worked hard for this. It's not fair to hold her back." She paused. Was she waiting for me to say I told you so? I had no words. And if I did, they wouldn't be the ones I'd choose.

She moved forward in her chair, her eyes searching my face. "I know you've been telling me this for years. I'm sorry I didn't listen."

I nodded. I needed to be honest with her now that she was listening. How could we work through things if we hid our thoughts and feelings? And that's one thing I needed to change. I needed to be braver and speak my mind. I had, for many years I had. And then as the drought set in and Taylor started spending less time with us, I felt like I'd lost my voice.

I stood and moved around to the front of the desk and sat on the edge. "I'm worried that you're saying all of this because my mother is here. That it won't last in the long term."

Taylor held my gaze as she stood and moved in close. "Maybe it was the wake up call I needed. Maybe it made me think about what I was doing wrong."

I reached for her hands and held them tight. Hers were clammy. Fuck, this was scary. I'd moved halfway around the world for her without even the slightest hesitation. We'd been together for over twenty years. I knew how good it could be, but I also knew how bad. If this didn't work, bad could be worse. But if I didn't try, why did I get married in the first place? Through the good and bad, right?

She smiled. "Maybe Mum telling me to pull my head out of my arse helped."

I laughed.

She moved in closer, nudging her way between my legs. "So, the other night when we were reminiscing with the kids, you skimmed over our first kiss."

Heat travelled through me. This is not how I imagined this meeting going.

"There are some things our children don't need to hear," I said.

"Maybe we should recreate it."

"Are you feeling cold?" My voice was husky.

I pulled her in closer. She wrapped her arms around my neck. As soon as our lips met, I was lost in her like I'd been that first day. Our lips moved in unison; every movement was more desperate than the last. I grabbed her arse, pulling her closer at the same time I pushed my hard dick against her. I wanted her more today than I had that first day. Because today I knew exactly what it felt like when I was inside her. And fuck, it was good.

I slipped my tongue in, probing hers. Her moan vibrated through me. I untucked her shirt and my hands slid up her back to her bra which I unclasped in record time. I ran my right hand under the material, moving it around to the front, finding her breast and squeezing it. Taylor's lips paused. She gasped, and I captured her rushed breath with my mouth. My dick got harder. I didn't even know it was possible.

"Taylor," I murmured. There were more words running around my head like wild horses but I couldn't catch them.

She pulled away. Her breaths were shaky. "I don't remember you doing that the first time."

"I wanted to see if perfection could be improved upon."

She stepped away. Her face was flushed as she did her bra up and tucked her shirt back in.

I raised my eyebrows. "Well?"

"It's fair to say my panties are wet." She looked between my legs at my obvious hard-on and smirked. "I don't need to ask if it was good for you."

"I wonder what else we can improve upon."

It had been a long time since we'd been intimate, months before our breakup. I was lonely in the marriage and lonely in bed.

"I wonder." She spun around and walked out, right

through the open door. A millisecond later she reappeared and with a sultry smile, said, "I look forward to it."

~

I MET the kids as they pulled into the carport.

"Is she here?" Isabelle asked as she threw her door open.

I nodded. "Aye. Inside, ready and waiting."

She yanked her bag out of the backseat and rushed off ahead. Callum soon followed.

"Isabelle. Callum," Mam called out in her strong Dublin accent.

"Mamo," Isabelle said as she embraced her.

Mam grabbed Callum and pulled him into their hug. She drew away and studied them both, smoothing down their hair. "It has been too long. You look prettier in person." She brushed her fingers across Callum's cheeks. "You have freckles like your mother."

"It's all the sun," Isabelle joked. "Not like Ireland."

Mam looked out the window. "It's not that warm here today."

Callum laughed. "It's the middle of winter."

"Aye. Tell me everything. How is school? What are you studying? How are your horses?"

They sat down beside each other on the couch. I made some coffees and hot chocolate and sat down opposite them. I had to give Taylor credit; she may not have gotten on that well with Mam, but she never did anything to change the kids' perception. She let them have the relationship they needed with her.

"Where's Taylor?" Mam asked.

Isabelle looked down at her feet. It wasn't only me Taylor had to prove herself to. Mam glanced at her sideways.

"She'll be here soon. She's gone to see if Lorraine can help tomorrow so the kids and I can spend the day with you."

Mam beamed. Isabelle lifted her eyes, and I gave her a reassuring smile. As we talked, I glanced at my watch. Taylor was later than I expected. Perhaps she'd got caught up at work. It wouldn't be the first time. When I heard her car pull up and her laughing with Lorraine, my shoulders relaxed. Isabelle was the same. She had been listening and waiting the whole time.

Taylor and Lorraine walked in. Lorraine went to the kitchen with a casserole dish. "We've made dinner."

That explained Taylor's delayed return. I stood and led the way to the dining table. As Taylor sat beside me, I wanted to lean over to give her a kiss but I restrained myself. I couldn't let the kids see it yet. They watched us all through dinner and spoke quietly together at times. I didn't know if that was because they were seeing changes in Taylor and me and the way we interacted, or they were planning another surprise they shouldn't be.

Mam was yawning by the end of dinner. I drove her and Lorraine home. I was tired too, but at the same time I was anxious about the conversation I needed to have with Taylor. I had no idea how she was going to react. This would be another conversation we'd have in the safety of darkness.

I hopped into bed and stared up at the ceiling. "Mam was excited that I'm spending the day with her tomorrow. Thank you."

Taylor turned her face to me. "You're welcome."

I continued to stare at the ceiling. Moonlight filtered in around the curtains, so it wasn't pitch black. I took a deep breath in and out. I didn't know where to start.

"Thank you for coming home early."

"That's what spending more time with you all means."

Was she being flippant?

"When we were waiting for you, Mam asked where you were, and Isabelle didn't know what to say."

Taylor was still facing me in the darkness. "What did you say?"

"That you were rearranging your day for tomorrow." I closed my eyes. This wasn't what I was expecting. This shouldn't be about what I'd said, but about how the kids were feeling. I needed to get that message across. "I think maybe you should speak to the kids. Tell them that you're going to start trying to spend more time at home."

"OK." The word was drawn out. I couldn't tell if she was considering what I said or if she was being defensive. "I guess that's a good idea."

That was positive.

I didn't know how long it was going to take for us to get back to a place of talking without fear. From the day we'd met, we'd spoken so openly. We'd never hedged our words, but as we'd drifted apart, the words became harder to say. I thought marriage was supposed to take those barriers away. It probably did for most people.

I relaxed a little. "I think it will help them see that you're making an effort." Shit, did that sound bad? Might as well get the rest out in the open: be brave. "It might be a good idea not to tell them we are trying to work things out. I don't want to raise their expectations or confuse them."

She stiffened. "Don't you think we can?"

Of course, I did. But one mind-blowing kiss wasn't going to miraculously fix things, nor were promises we made to each other. We'd made those same promises twenty-two years ago and then we'd fallen apart.

"I think we should take our time," I said. "We didn't get

to where we are overnight. We don't need the extra pressure of their expectations."

"So you think we can?" Her voice was small, uncertain. A tone I hadn't heard since the day we'd met.

I reached out and grabbed her hand. I faced her then so she could see my truth. "Nothing would make me happier."

She smiled. "I love you, Ciaron. I never stopped. I just forgot to show it."

And that wasn't entirely on her.

"Me too. We can do this Taylor. Together we can do anything."

"Yes, we can."

We fell asleep holding each other's hand. Tonight, the promises were enough. Tomorrow and every day after that we'd need to work on making them real.

16

Taylor

I ran my hand through my hair as I stared at the computer. This shit was hard. Ciaron dealt with as many competing priorities as me. He never seemed bothered by it, and everything flowed smoothly.

I'd forgotten that he'd taken on as much extra work as I had. How did he manage it all and keep on top of all our family responsibilities? Maybe because he didn't hide behind it all like me. Dread spread through my body. My muscles were so heavy it was an effort to move. I'd done that. I'd hidden behind work. I didn't want to admit that everything was out of control, so I controlled work to the nth degree.

I was in the middle of checking an order for first-aid materials and thinking about the list of jobs Ciaron had left me, including checking the birthing aids, when I heard a call on the two-way about an injured horse. The stud hand asked for Ciaron. She must have forgotten he was away.

I picked up the two-way. "This is Taylor. Ciaron is on leave today. Lorraine or I can help."

"I have an injured horse in the Bottom Road Paddock."

"OK. Be there soon."

I made my way down to the paddock and turned onto the road after Mum, sitting back a little as the dust flew up from the dry road. We really should have decided which one of us would go. Too late now. We got out of our cars and headed over to the horse and the two stud hands.

"I was showing Sofia the different paddocks, and we noticed Mermaid limping," Cleo said.

I was a few metres away from Mermaid and I could already tell a vet was needed. The skin on her shoulder was torn away. A flap about the size of a hand hung down. She'd be in a considerable amount of pain.

"Can you get the truck, Mum? We need to get her to the hospital barn."

She nodded and left the paddock.

I turned to the two stud hands. "Can you please check the fences and look for any low-lying branches that could have caused this?"

They headed off. Of course, Mermaid could have been kicked by another horse as well. But if there was a problem out there in the paddock, we needed to fix it so another horse wasn't injured.

Mermaid stood beside me quietly as I called the vet. I patted her neck. Then I watched the stud hands while I waited for the truck. I should have told them they'd done a good job spotting the injury. Ciaron would have done that almost straight away, and he would have thanked them. Now, they were too far away.

I examined the injury closer. It wasn't very deep, thankfully. It was fresh too. The skin wasn't drying out yet, which meant stitching would be viable. I handed the horse off to Mum when she arrived. "Call me when the vet arrives, please."

I headed out to the two stud hands who were walking the fence line. "Have you found anything?"

"No, nothing."

"OK. Thanks. Good job on spotting the injury."

Cleo smiled. "It was weird that she wasn't with the herd."

It was noticing small things like that that made a good stud hand.

"Finish the fence line and if you can't find anything, head back to work. Let me know either way, please."

"OK."

I grabbed my phone out to call Mermaid's owners. I needed to let them know about her injury and that she required vet treatment. I hated this part of the job. It was another thing Ciaron was good at. He had a great rapport with our clients. It was something I had been more involved in before Mum had retired. I needed to get back into it; our clients were important, as were their horses.

Ciaron did so much that I didn't give him credit for. And all of it made my job as general manager easier. I'd forgotten we were a team.

I headed back to the office to continue the paperwork. My fingers were brown from patting Mermaid and there was dirt under my nails. No rain meant no natural baths for the horses. When Mum called, I made my way to the hospital barn.

Dan, the vet, looked up and grinned as I walked in, his grey hair shining in the light. "Oooh, we have the big boss today."

"Aren't you lucky?"

"Where's Ciaron? Did you let him off the ball and chain?"

"I decided he'd earnt a day of freedom."

Mum laughed. "Only a day."

Dan examined the wound. He uncurled his wiry, tall body. He was still spritely for a sixty-something year old. "It looks pretty clean. No real tissue damage. It will just need a flush and a lot of stitches."

"Good."

He started cleaning the wound. "Is Isabelle looking forward to her work experience with us next month?"

"Sure is."

I hoped I sounded convincing. I didn't even know she had work experience coming up.

"She will get to come on rounds with me and watch some surgeries as well."

"Excellent."

"Ciaron told me if she got stuck doing generic shit, he'd make sure I was called to flush the mares out."

Mum laughed. "That man has a way of convincing people."

Dan chuckled. "He convinced Taylor to marry him in less than twenty-four hours."

"In my defence, I thought he was joking." For the first few hours, that is. After that first night, I knew he was serious.

"And then he followed you all the way here," Mum said.

Gosh, I'd missed him while I waited for him to get here. It had been like I was an eventing horse with no obstacles to jump. "I couldn't deny him after that, could I?"

"Hell no," Dan said. "Dedication like that should be rewarded."

Up until our split, I thought we'd been dedicated to each

other, but my dedication had strayed. I thought saving the farm was important for my family, but what they really wanted was me. I'd had it all wrong in my head. I wasn't going to give up on the farm. It had survived many natural disasters. But if I had to choose, I'd choose Ciaron and my children.

Dan stood straight. "All done."

I looked at the wound. It was a neat stitch job.

"Thanks."

"Give her oral antibiotics twice a day for a week. Keep her in a yard to restrict her ability to run."

"OK."

"Back to the subject of dedication." He faced Mum. "Are you ready to go on a date with me yet?"

My head whipped in Mum's direction. He'd been dedicated to asking her out for the last twenty years. They had a great rapport and joked with each other all the time. I knew they liked each other because they'd often speak or ask about the other. I never understood why she kept saying no.

She gave him a sly smile. "You can be my date for Isabelle's party."

"Finally." He grinned and did a happy dance. "It's only taken twenty years for you to say yes."

"Persistence pays off," she said.

Interesting. Why had she said yes after all these years of denying him?

When he left, Mum said, "You didn't know Isabelle was doing her work experience at the vet surgery?"

I shook my head. "I'm really failing at parenting. Ciaron handled it all. He probably told me."

"It seems to me that he handles a lot of things."

I rubbed my hand over my face. "I've been taking him for granted."

"It's probably easy to do with someone who takes everything on without complaint."

I nodded. "Can you let Mermaid out? I need to ring her owner."

"Sure. I'll see you at dinner."

I headed to the door.

"Taylor," Mum said.

I turned around.

"If you need help to pay for the party, it can be my gift to Isabelle. I know money is tight at the moment."

"Thanks, Mum."

I headed back to the office, not thinking about the party, but Ciaron.

Ciaron did so much more than most men would. He took on my dreams about the farm and made them his own. He never considered our future as anything else but this. For him, it had always been about us. There wasn't him as an individual anymore. And he didn't complain about it. He didn't complain about anything. All he wanted was more us.

For twenty-two years, his love had never swayed.

He gave us *everything* and I forgot to give us *anything*.

I was such a hypocrite. I'd been frustrated with Mary when Ciaron told me how much he'd done while growing up. She let him do everything that she should have been doing. She was the parent, not him. He was a child looking after other children because she was more interested in the next man in her life.

And now, I was no better. The only difference was it wasn't because of a man.

CIARON STOPPED *in front of a wooden door of a brown brick building. The building was two-storey, just like the one next to it and the one after that. It was the same all the way down the street. And every door was right on the footpath. There was no yard. I stood behind him, wiping my sweaty palms on my jeans. He swung the door open and faced me.*

"Ready?"

"Yep." I smiled as much as my nerves would allow.

He stepped through the door. I followed. Shoes were scattered in the small entry. He kicked them out of the way.

"Sorry. It got a bit messy in the three days I've been away."

The three days we'd spent together since we'd met.

Was it his job to tidy up after everyone? Maybe that was one of his responsibilities. At home, Mum cooked, I did the dishes. We shared the cleaning.

A young boy ran into the hallway, followed by an older one. "Give it back to me, you fucking little shit."

"Will you stop fighting?" a female voice called from further in the house. "I'm sick of hearing it."

The two boys stopped in front of Ciaron, who held out his hand. The younger one passed over a remote. That's when he noticed me. Ciaron placed his hand on my back.

"Tommy, Seamus, this is Taylor."

"Hi," I said.

"Mam, Ciaron's home," the older boy yelled.

Footsteps rushed towards us. "About time. Where have you been?"

I took the time to study her. She was tall and slim with dyed blonde hair. Her cheeks were flushed. She continued to talk as she made her way down the hall. "Tommy needs help with his homework, and Ronan needs to be picked up from practice. I can't do everything."

My jaw clenched. It was her job to look after her *children, not Ciaron's. I held my tongue. It was hard.*

Ciaron's hand stiffened. His whole body stiffened. In three days, I'd never seen him so tense, even with my father. I squeezed his hand, and he relaxed.

His mother stopped short when she saw me. A hint of alcohol wafted in the air. She smoothed down her black top and then widened her eyes at Ciaron.

"Mam, this is Taylor. Taylor, my mam, Mary."

"Nice to meet you, Mary."

"Is that where you've been for three days?" Mary said, staring pointedly at me. "What about work?"

I moved closer to Ciaron. Obviously, Mary didn't think it was nice to meet me.

"I spoke to work. I had some time owing to me."

She grunted. "You spoke to work, but you couldn't manage to speak to me."

"The phone has been disconnected," Ciaron said. "I'm not sure why since I gave you money for it last week."

She scowled "Don't f—."

"Ciaron wanted me to meet you before I left," I said, interrupting her. "We'll be getting married in Australia."

We hadn't really spoken about when we were going to get married. I didn't actually think he was serious until he'd got a tattoo with my name. So we discussed that he was going to apply for a passport and as soon as he got it, he'd be selling his car and buying a one-way plane ticket.

Ciaron smiled down at me.

"Married?" Mary asked.

I moved closer to Ciaron and put my arm around his waist. I wanted to say 'so he can get away from you' but instead said, "Yes."

"That's cause for celebration, I suppose," she said. *She gazed up at him and stroked his hair, not caring that her arm was in my face. Ciaron's brothers stared at her before screwing their faces up. As she turned to walk down the hallway, she looked back over her shoulder and gave me a smile. It felt like I'd been slapped in the face with slime.*

We followed her into the kitchen/dining room. There was a table squished into the corner. Ciaron directed me to a seat as his mother got some glasses out, poured Guinness into them, and put them on the table. Ciaron went to sit in the seat next to me, but Mary shoved one of the brothers into it. She pulled Ciaron away to the other end of the table to sit next to her. Ciaron's brothers asked me lots of questions while she sat there tight-lipped and rigid.

I had no doubt that she'd try to convince him to change his mind right until he hopped on that flight. I wondered if his father would be the same. We were going to visit him next.

Mary hadn't been able to change his mind. He was in Australia working with Mum and me on the farm within two months. He'd moved half a world away to be with me and I should have been more appreciative.

Enough with taking him for granted. Not just for the things he did everyday but for him. For the man he was, the man who loved us, his kindness, his humility. Him.

17

Ciaron

We sat in the lounge room, resting after our day touring. The kids had wanted to show Mam their school and some of the other studs. We'd had lunch out as well. Mam seemed shocked at our isolation. I didn't notice it. We had everything we needed close by and more shops within half an hour. We didn't need everything a city like Dublin had.

She was happy when the bottle shop stocked her favourite beer. I guess that made up for our living in the country.

It was important to spend local, especially in times of natural disasters like a drought. It's what kept the community going. We all needed each other. If these businesses closed, we'd need to travel further and we'd lose connection. Farmers and businesses may not see each other on a daily, weekly or even monthly basis, but if help was needed, we'd be there for one another.

"What time will Taylor get home?" Mam asked. She'd

seemed to pick up that this was a sore point. Maybe she'd seen Isabelle's response to it yesterday. She'd also mentioned something earlier in the day to gauge our reactions.

"I'm sure she won't be much longer," I said. "She texted before to say she had to check on an injured horse on the way home."

The text was a welcome surprise. Normally, we were left waiting. It was these little things that showed me she was listening.

"Do you want us to start dinner, Dad?" Callum asked.

"Sure. Shepherd's Pie."

Isabelle followed Callum into the kitchen.

"Even though both of you are cooking, it only counts as one meal," I said.

Mam raised her eyebrows.

"They each have to cook one meal a week," I explained.

She nodded. I wonder if she thought back to when I was their age and cooked most meals. It was either that or my brothers and I would go hungry.

Taylor's car pulled into the driveway. As soon as she walked in the door, she threw me a smile. My heart lifted. It had been a long time since she'd smiled when she came home. Just the lifting of her lips changed her whole demeanour. I'd missed it.

She spotted the kids in the kitchen. "Do you need any help?"

"No way. If you help, it won't qualify as our meal," Isabelle said.

Taylor sat beside me on the couch. She sighed as she leant back.

"Long day?" I asked.

She nodded. "Hard work without you there."

I laughed. "It was only one day."

"I know. But I forgot how much you do."

I tried not to show my shock. Sometimes I felt she thought what I did was insignificant.

Mam moved closer and put her hand on my leg. "It's good you notice that Ciaron is such a hard worker."

Did she mean that she recognised how much work I did when I was younger as well?

Taylor glanced between Mam and me. "How was your day?"

"Wonderful," Mam said. "I enjoyed spending the day with my boy."

"What did you do?" Taylor asked.

I tried not to smile at how she was so obvious about ignoring Mam's statement. She'd always hated the obtuse way Mam tried to claim me. I was impressed she didn't roll her eyes.

We spoke about our days as the kids cooked and then, through dinner, we got updates about the family back in Ireland. I knew everything about my brothers. We always kept in contact, but not so much about the extended family. Mam avoided speaking about Dad, who'd retired from his life of crime and had moved to another city with a woman he'd met while in jail. I was happy for him. I only wish he'd left the toxic relationship with Mam sooner and then maybe she would have been happier.

Maybe even had more time to love us.

After I drove Mam home, Taylor and I did the dishes together.

"Thank you for filling in for me today," I said as she placed the last plate into the dish rack.

I kissed her cheek. Now that the kids were in bed, I was able to touch her. And I didn't want to stop at a simple kiss.

"You're welcome." She put the dish cloth down and turned to me and then held eye contact. "Thank you for everything you do every day at work, at home, with the children."

"That's my job."

She shook her head. "No. That's *our* job."

What was going on here? One day in my shoes and she was saying the words I'd wanted to hear months ago? I couldn't understand why she'd waited until now to say these things.

She reached up and pushed hair out of my face. Her fingers lingered on my cheek. "I'm sorry I forgot we were a team. You kept giving, and I kept taking."

My throat tightened.

"I never wanted to be like your mother. But somehow, I was. I'm sorry."

She laid her hand on my cheek, and I covered it with mine before I moved my head to the left so I could kiss it.

"You're not like her, Taylor. You're here standing in front of me, recognising your faults and apologising for them. My mother has never done that."

Her eyes filled with tears.

"I was wrong too." I took her free hand. "I gave and gave and didn't say anything until I got angry. By that time, we were separate teams. I should have spoken up earlier."

I searched her eyes. She stared right back. I needed to tell her what I'd done. How in the end I'd given away my decision making.

"I let you handle the money because I worked on the farm and I handled everything outside of work and I was sick of it," I said.

She took a shaky breath. "How did we get here, Ciaron? I never thought we'd be these people."

"Maybe we forgot we still needed to work for us."

"Not maybe, we did."

I nodded. "We did."

I wrapped her in my arms. We weren't where we needed to be yet, but we were closer than I thought we'd ever be. And if we didn't love each other, we wouldn't have gotten this far. Maybe love was enough.

18

Taylor

I sat in the morning meeting listening to Ciaron. I hadn't been attending morning meetings as much as I should have, preferring to get on with the day's work. It meant we were not presenting as a united team. Another casualty of our failing relationship.

"This morning we're going to move some paddocks. The ones at the top road I'd like to move down to the river paddock," Ciaron said.

I shifted in my seat. That didn't make sense. I was sure those horses were due first. So why were we moving them further away from the foaling unit? That was a mistake. If one went into labour out in that paddock, we wouldn't be able to move them quick enough. They could give birth before we even got to them. A mare's labour could last less than fifteen minutes.

I bit my lip. Now was not the time to bring it up. He was the broodmare manager and where horses moved to was up to him. He didn't need to consult me about it. Ciaron paused, his gaze stopped on me as he glanced around the room. I trained my face into a neutral look.

After the meeting I drove past the paddock Ciaron was planning to move. The horses there were definitely the ones who were due first. I waited for Ciaron to get back to the office and then made my way to him. He looked up from his desk when I came in.

I sat before I said anything. I didn't want him to feel like I was standing over the top of him. "That paddock of horses we're moving. They're due first. Should we keep them closer to the foaling unit?"

Ciaron shook his head. "They haven't had fresh grass for a while. This will be their last chance."

"Is it worth the risk?" I pressed.

"None of them have started to show signs. And at least four of them don't usually birth early or on time." His answer came quick. It was obvious he'd thought about it in depth because he'd checked and done his research.

"OK. That makes sense."

"Thank you for waiting until I came back before asking about my reasoning."

I smiled. "See, I do listen."

Ciaron cracked a grin. "Wonders will never cease."

I shook my head in jest. "Don't push your luck."

He laughed. "I'd never dream of it."

Gosh, I'd missed that laugh. I missed so much about him. Most of all, I missed my best friend.

He studied me. "Does that mean you're ready to discuss the breeding choices for this season?"

"I thought you'd never ask."

And that was the truth. I thought he'd lost interest in the farm as well as me.

"I wanted to, but you didn't seem to want to share anything."

He wasn't lying. The more lost I felt outside of work, the closer I held everything at work.

"I know. I'm sorry."

I looked down at my hands in my lap. I had so much to be sorry for. How were we ever going to get back to where we were—happy and strong? Were we past full repair, like if we were to fix things, we'd be fragile and ready to break with just the slightest stress?

"Taylor."

Could we ever be us again?

How could he love me after the way I treated him? I was as bad as his mother, the way I just expected him to do everything. I forgot to consider his feelings. Then I'd accused him of being unfaithful like his parents. I couldn't get past these mistakes. My mistakes. How could he?

"Taylor."

I raised my eyes to Ciaron, but he was no longer in his seat. He was crouched beside me. He moved in front of me and placed his hands on my thighs. "It's OK to recognise what we did wrong, but we can't hold on to blame."

He was always too forgiving. His mam. Me. Was it because he didn't love himself enough?

"You deserve better, Ciaron."

Ciaron stood up and pulled me with him. "What, and you don't?"

"I'm the one that broke us."

"We broke us, Taylor. *We* did. There were two of us in this marriage. And there were two of us out of it."

My hands were shaking in his. "You tried to tell me more than once that we had a problem."

"Yeah, well, maybe I should have tried harder earlier. Maybe I should have told you before it all turned to shit instead of trying to smooth it all over." He cupped my face and searched my eyes. "I will never make that mistake again. I love you, Taylor. Now. Today. Forever."

He bent his head forward and kissed me. His warm hands framed my face as his fingers entwined in my hair. I breathed in his scent—man, horse and earthiness. Pure aphrodisiac.

My stomach swirled.

"Wait here," Ciaron said. He walked to his office door, pressed the lock in and closed it. "We don't need everyone hearing us making up."

I giggled. "What does making up involve?"

Ciaron stood in front of me and held my chin. "Maybe this." His tongue swept across my lower lip. He pressed himself against me and warmth spread between my legs and settled in my core.

"And maybe this." He kissed me hard and wet while his hands went to the button on my jeans. His fingers were hectic as he struggled with the button and zip. He pulled my jeans down below my arse.

"This." He slipped his hand into my underwear. His fingers circled around my clit. A small cry escaped my lips as I pushed myself against his hand. His hot breaths against my cheek were ragged. Fuck, he was so turned on. My breaths matched his. He pushed his fingers in and then dragged them back out, rubbing against my swollen clit. My legs shook.

I moaned.

"You're going to come on my hand and then on my dick," Ciaron rasped out.

His fingers were rough, insistent, probing. My toes curled in my steel cap boots.

"That's it," he groaned. "Come for me."

His fingers were deliberate, coaxing me. I clutched at his shoulders as my legs gave way. I clenched my teeth and came undone. Ciaron covered my lips with his, drowning out my cry. His fingers slowed, matching my trembles and luring more out of me.

My panting slowed as my muscles relaxed. Ciaron and I were cheek to cheek. His lifted in a smile. "I'm enjoying this making up."

I nodded, unable to form words as I released my fingers from his shoulders. Ciaron spun me around and pulled my underwear down. He lowered his zip and his jeans rustled as he pushed them down. My stomach squeezed as his hand wrapped firmly around my hip. The perfect fit. He moved in close. His breath brushed my ear, sending heat and a shiver through me.

"Try not to let Fran hear how much you love my dick inside you." His voice was husky and just that alone kept me on the brink of orgasm.

I blushed. The only reason Fran hadn't heard me cry out was because Ciaron had absorbed it with his mouth.

"Maybe you shouldn't have made me come so hard."

Ciaron chuckled. "Time for round two."

"Show me what you got, Irish Boy."

I scanned the window. The wooden venetians were slightly open, letting light in. But no one would be out there gardening. So, there would be no one to accidentally see us.

He tilted my hips and guided himself inside me. I leant forward, resting my hands on his desk. It was cold for a moment before the heat in my palms transferred. Holy shit. The stretch. It kept coming and felt so good. Ciaron's other hand came to my hip, holding tight. He tilted my arse. After twenty years, he knew exactly how to hit the spot. We moaned in unison. I flattened my palms on the desktop and pushed myself back against him. The only question left was who would orgasm first.

19

Ciaron

I glided in and out of Taylor. She squeezed her pussy around my dick, increasing the friction like she did our first time.

Fuck. My fingers tightened, digging into her flesh.

I held her in place as I increased my rhythm. Every stroke drove me closer. I adjusted my grip so I could open her wider and I thrust deeper. A small whimper escaped her lips. The sound said she was begging me for more. I loved the control I had in this moment.

My balls tightened.

"Fuck," I gritted out.

I couldn't come yet. Not until I could feel her shaking beneath me. If she didn't come as hard as she'd done with my fingers inside her, I wasn't doing it right.

I was so fucking close. So was she.

Taylor's fingers stretched and tensed. A moan escaped. She needed to come soon before I exploded. I drove in and out and watched her back arch. Then she spasmed around my dick.

My clenched teeth could not contain my groan. My balls tightened. My whole body shuddered.

Taylor cried out. I covered her mouth with my hand, dulling the sound. Desperation surged in me. I thrust deep and hard, and then stilled as I emptied myself inside her. Jerk after jerk shocked my body.

I pulled away slowly, and Taylor stood, unsteady. Sweaty handprints remained on my desk. I held her against me, our chests heaving in harmony.

"Kissing and making up just took on a whole new meaning," I said into her hair.

Taylor glanced at the locked door. "I don't think I can go out there for a while. You were so loud." She giggled.

"I was loud? I had to cover your mouth so the whole farm couldn't hear your cry." I kissed her hair. "Lucky we still have to talk about the breeding for this season. We can stay in here a bit longer."

"Shame the horses don't enjoy sex as much as we do."

"Such a waste."

I moved away and pulled up my jeans, smiling to myself. It had been a while since we'd had sex in the office. And fuck, that was hot. I might have to take her up against the door next time, to test how quiet she could be. Next time. I had no doubt there would be one. Her promise to me meant we were building our future, but what we had just done cemented it.

Taylor sat back in the chair. I sat at my desk, turned my monitor so we could both see it and started our discussion. Every now and then I glanced at the handprints on my wooden desktop. My mind would flash back to Taylor bent over it and my dick inside her. A smile would creep out. And I'm sure if my dick wasn't still recovering, it would twitch.

We spoke about our mares, the client mares and the stallions standing at stud. We didn't have any control over the client mares, but as part of our service to them, we would collate and present suggestions. Once they made a decision, we would make the bookings.

I let go of the mouse. "Happy with what we have for the clients?"

"Yes. I'll call them tomorrow and then email."

I tilted my head. "You'll call?"

"Yes. It's my job as general manager. You started to take it on, and I let you, but I shouldn't have."

And I hadn't pushed back, like with everything else. That was part of our problem. I never pushed back.

"I don't know why I did that," I said.

Taylor gave me a gentle smile. "I don't know why I let you."

This discussion was good. We had so much we needed to improve on. The fact that we could talk about it without accusations and resentment was important. It was better than where we'd been a few weeks ago, where even when we were trying to be nice, snideness would slip out.

"Maybe if we weren't married, it would have been different," she said.

I tensed. "What do you mean?"

"If we had just been business partners, we probably would have held each other to account more often."

I relaxed my jaw. "True. We would have had more respect for boundaries."

"We didn't have that here or at home."

I shook my head. "No, we didn't."

"If I invested as much time in our relationship and our family as I did the farm, we wouldn't be in this situation."

"But we may not have the farm if you didn't."

It was a fact I had to face. One that she needed to face too. If it came to it, would she be willing to give the farm and her family legacy up? We weren't at that point yet, but we could get there. And if we did, would she actually be able to do it?

She held my gaze. "It's a piece of land, a business. I love it, yes. But I love you and the children more."

My chest lightened. "I don't want to lose the farm, Taylor. I love it here. I love what we have built up. But I don't want to save the farm and lose us."

"Me either."

I reached my hand out. She took it.

"It's time for us to save both," I said.

She grinned. "Does that involve you showing me a good time?"

"Like before?" I waggled my eyebrows.

"Yes."

"There will be so many good times it will be like a party."

My dick would be dancing for joy.

She let go of my hand, her eyes wide. "Party. Shit. Do you know what Isabelle has planned?"

"No bloody idea. But as her mother, I think you should figure that out."

"Nice play, Irish Boy."

"Do I get rewarded with a kiss?"

"You'll have to come and get it."

I rounded the desk and pulled her up out of her chair. As soon as my lips met hers, they opened and moved in unison. Her tongue stroked mine and my whole body remembered our first kiss and everything that had followed.

But that everything hadn't all been good, at least in the last twelve months. And deep, deep down, the reminder nipped at me. I shoved it away like I would a naughty horse. It didn't need to be here when we were both trying so hard communicating and opening up to each other in a way we hadn't done in so long.

20

Taylor

It was dark by the time Ciaron and I got home. When we walked in together, the kids were cooking with Mary. Isabelle did not give me her usual irritated look because I was late. Funny that. It seemed like it was OK for me to be late if I was with Ciaron, but not if it was me alone.

"Ciaron, can you swap with Isabelle, please? We need to get some birthday stuff organised," I said.

Isabelle's eyes widened. She washed her hands and dried them hesitantly. Then she joined me in the lounge room.

"What plans do you have for your party?" I asked her.

She glanced at Callum, who was too busy to notice.

"It must be something special seeing you have both grandmothers here."

She clasped her hands in her lap. "I didn't really plan anything beyond that."

"So your grand plan was to get them here in the hope of what, getting your dad and I back together?"

She pursed her lips. "Yeah."

Why would she think Mary would help with that plan? Because there was no way Mary would ever help put us together if she knew she could tear us apart. How could I ask Isabelle without sounding rude?

"What was Mamo's part to play in this?"

"Dad can only stand her in short bursts. Remember what it was like when we visited Ireland a few years ago?"

I nodded, although I was surprised she could recall what it was like. She was ten at the time and I'd tried to shelter her from any negativity. We'd stayed with one of Ciaron's brothers under the premise that it would be good for the kids to spend time with their cousins. And we didn't spend an extended amount of time with Mary. One of many incidents came to mind. One where she managed to have a go at me yet again. One of the many times I should have stood up to her over the years.

We sat around the table eating lunch at Ronan's house. Seamus's girlfriend was clearing the table and loading the dishwasher. I went to help her, but Ciaron told me he wanted to do it. He wanted to have a quiet talk to her about Seamus. He had a feeling he was getting into trouble. And he wanted to use his brotherly powers to determine if she was leading him astray.

Mary watched the exchange between us with interest. My skin crawled. I ignored her the best I could. Seamus was her son. She should have been the one checking in on him. But we knew she wasn't. When Ciaron walked off, she said to Ronan's wife, "Ciaron was always the best out of my boys. Then he went off to Australia and left us all to fend for ourselves."

Ciaron's steps faltered, and his head dropped. I shifted in my seat. Imagine saying that in front of your other children. A parent shouldn't have favourites and even if they did, they shouldn't pronounce it like that. And it wasn't Ciaron's job to fend for all of them. He was also her child.

The boys all had different reactions, from shaking heads to swearing under their breath. They were like horses chomping at the bit. Ciaron wouldn't have said anything if it was just about himself, but it wasn't.

Ciaron faced Mary. "I wouldn't say I was the best. Tommy got top marks in school. Ronan was best and fairest year after year in football. Seamus always made us laugh. And Billy was the first of us to buy a house."

Mary smiled her fake, placid smile. "Yes, yes. I meant at home."

Everyone knew she said it to save herself. Ciaron continued to the kitchen.

"I'll never understand what's so good about Australia," Mary whispered loudly as he walked away.

Ronan's wife stared at me wide eyed. I turned my attention to the boys.

Because she didn't get the reaction she wanted, she added, "He could have had his pick of good Irish women here, found one that would fit in better." She snickered. "I'm sure he'll come home soon. He'll realise his mistake."

I closed my eyes. That woman was a complete bitch. Only five days left before we went back home, and I couldn't wait.

ISABELLE SHIFTED IN HER SEAT, bringing my attention back to her. "Well, we figured if Dad had to spend a lot of time with Mamo, it would turn him off wanting to go back to Ireland."

They were more cunning than I gave them credit for. I didn't tell her that their plan for us to get back together was working. Ciaron and I hadn't discussed further about whether we were going to tell Callum and Isabelle that we were trying to reconcile. I didn't want to tell her until we agreed. It wasn't a good idea to play with their feelings.

"Nice plan," I said. "But I think Mamo is going to get suspicious if we don't do something."

"I guess."

I rested my hand on her leg, hoping she would find it reassuring. She didn't move away.

"Maybe we can do something small with us and some close friends. What do you think?"

"Yeah. OK."

"We can have it in the staff dining room. Maybe order some pizzas."

She nodded. "That will make it easy. Dad won't have to spend all day cooking."

And it would be cheaper. We didn't have to buy from the most expensive range of pizzas; the value range would suffice.

"Nanna said she would help pay as part of your birthday present."

Isabelle's shoulders relaxed. I hated knowing that she was thinking of the expense.

"It will be easy to clean up too," I said. "Is there anyone you want to invite? Nanna has invited vet Dan for their first date."

Isabelle giggled. "He told me yesterday that for every date he gets, he will pay me a day while on work experience."

I rolled my eyes. And held my laughter in. I can't believe he was bribing Isabelle to set him up with Mum. "Let's get them through this one first, huh?"

"At least that's one paid day," she said.

I glanced at Ciaron. He was watching us. My stomach

lifted when he gave me a smile. How on earth was I going to hide my feelings from the kids when I got giddy from a smile?

I turned back to Isabelle. "Would you like a theme for your party?"

Her mouth dropped open. "Should I?"

"You don't need to. It's been so long since we organised something together. I wasn't sure what you would want."

She bit her lip.

I kept my hand on her leg. "I'm sorry that I haven't been here for you when you needed me."

She gave a small shrug, but I could tell she was holding back tears. I swallowed the lump in my throat.

"I can't fix what's happened, but I can try to be a better mum."

She nodded.

I didn't know what that meant. That she wanted me to but didn't believe I could. Or that it would take more than one promise to rebuild our relationship. Or that she was happy I admitted I'd fucked up. It didn't matter. I had to prove that I was going to be a better mother, like I had been before it all started falling apart. And this was the start.

"OK. Figure out a list of names so we can get some invites out and I'll order pizza."

I didn't know who her friends were, so I didn't throw any names out there. What a disgusting thing to admit. It was those friends that would help shape her life. And by what had been said during parent-teacher interviews, she'd chosen better ones this year. I couldn't help but wonder if other working mums had this problem too. Most were probably like Ciaron. He had much more involvement than me.

"All sorted?" Ciaron asked as he set the table.

I stood and went to help him. "Getting there. Just a couple of last-minute things."

He gave my hand a squeeze. I held on for a moment longer than necessary. I wanted him to know I appreciated his support.

We sat down for dinner, Ciaron and I next to each other as usual and the kids opposite us. Mary sat next to Ciaron, touching his arm and looking up at him whenever he spoke. I stabbed at my potatoes. I doubt she'd paid him this much attention to him growing up.

"Do you need us to help with dinner again tomorrow, Taylor?" Mary said. "Isabelle and Callum said you get home late a lot."

The tongs of my fork clinked on the plate. Isabelle and Callum shifted in their seats. I stared at the space between them. I didn't want them to feel bad for stating a fact, even though I wished they'd said it to anyone else but Mary.

"Ciaron usually does the cooking," I said.

"Oh."

I'm sure she knew that, but she'd still found a way to have a dig at me.

"Dad's a better cook," Callum said lightly.

Another pat on the arm from Mary.

"Mum makes the best spag bol though," Isabelle said.

I smiled at her and gave her a silent high-five.

"The agreement in our house is that one cooks, and the others do the dishes," Ciaron said. "I hate doing the dishes."

"Probably as much as Mum hates cooking," Callum said.

"That's why we are a perfect match." Ciaron lent over and gave me a kiss.

I tried to hide my surprise. Yes, we were trying to show Mary that we were still a strong couple in love. And that is exactly what we were working towards. But I didn't know we were going to be so open in front of the kids. Not when we'd agreed to shelter them from our healing until we were more certain.

Callum and Isabelle didn't miss the kiss, judging by the small grins on their faces. Neither did Mary, as evidenced by her not so quiet grunt. And just for her viewing pleasure, I gave him another one. I didn't care how petty it was. Or how poor Ciaron was feeling being stuck in the middle. He put himself there by kissing me first.

"Ciaron said earlier that Ireland is much better for farms like this," Mary said.

Did he just? Why would I want to leave the family farm to start another one in another country? To be closer to her? No, thank you.

I gave him a sidelong glance.

"What I said was that I'd sure like some of Ireland's rain right now," Ciaron said.

"Yes, yes, same thing. You wouldn't need to worry about droughts or bushfires."

I pressed my feet firmly onto the floor, directing my frustration there. "There was a drought in 2018."

"One year doesn't count for much of a drought. I think it would be easier for you both, and you wouldn't have to work so much, Taylor. You could be with your family more. I'm sure the children would like that."

Did Callum and Isabelle agree? I snuck a look at them both. Isabelle was frowning. My stomach dropped. I didn't want our talk earlier to be wiped out by Mary. I thought we'd made some progress.

If only stabbing someone wasn't illegal. Because I'd sure like to stab her with my fork right now.

"Farms are hard work everywhere, Mam," Ciaron said, almost like it was an afterthought.

He wasn't wrong. But the delay in his answer made me wonder if he actually believed it. Maybe he thought farming in Ireland would be easier than here. For fuck's sake, everything that involved Mary had me overthinking, doubting, reacting. But I couldn't help it. I needed to, though. If I ruined these two weeks because of my attitude towards her, I could wipe out hope for our future.

21

Ciaron

Taylor was putting the last of the dishes away when I got back from dropping Mam off. Mam had changed since I was younger. She recognised my efforts more. She seemed to think Taylor was taking advantage of me sometimes and maybe she recognised that she was like that too. It felt like she was trying to help when mentioning how I always did the cooking.

"That was a fun dinner," I said.

Taylor gave me a withering look. "Fun for the golden child, perhaps."

I shrugged. "I can't help being amazing." I sidled up behind her and wrapped my arms around her. "Thank you for not giving it to her."

She turned in my arms. "Lucky, I love you."

I chuckled. "Or else I'd be stabbed with that fork instead of kissed on the cheek?"

"Yep." She gave me a soft kiss.

"How did your chat with Isabelle go?"

"Good. I think. I told her I was sorry and that I was going to do better."

"And what did she say?"

"Nothing really. I think she will be harder to win over than you."

I brushed her hair back with my fingertips.

"Actions speak louder than words. She did stick up for you at dinner, though."

Taylor rolled her eyes and shook her head. I knew she meant that it shouldn't have been necessary for her to do it.

"She did admit she had no plans for a party. It was all a ploy to get us back together."

I pulled her closer. "It worked."

She nodded and smiled. "We are going to organise a small pizza party, so your mam doesn't get suspicious." She rested her hands on my chest. "A party would be good for everyone; I think it would be good for morale."

"Good plan." I bent my head to hers and tugged at her bottom lip.

"You know what else is a good plan?" she asked as she ran her hands over my chest. She pushed herself against me.

"What?" I rasped out.

"We get naked and go shower," she whispered against my lips.

I grabbed her arse and pulled her against my hard-on. "We'll save water showering together."

"We can get all hot and sweaty and clean at the same time."

Fuck me if my dick didn't get harder. "Twice in one day." My voice was unsteady.

"Need to make up for all the good times we missed out on," she said, before she brushed her lips against my neck.

I held her close. "Is this how you're going to win me over?"

"Is it working?"

"Fuck yeah."

I pulled her along the hallway to our room, switching off the lights as we went. Taylor was already on her way to the shower before I stripped off my clothes and left them in a pile on the floor. She turned the water on and beckoned me in. I watched as she soaped herself up, running her hands over her body, massaging her breasts and teasing her nipples. I swallowed as I stared at her. Her hand drifted lower, rubbing circles on her stomach with the soap, bubbles emerging and disappearing within moments. She glided over her hips and over her small birthmark. Her hand slipped between her legs.

The way she watched me watching her was seductive. Her teeth grazed her lip. A tremor ran through me. My dick pulsated as she sighed. Only a small sigh. I wanted to beat my chest, knowing she'd only given herself a little bit of pleasure compared to the hot orgasm I'd given her earlier.

She handed the soap to me, her fingers lingering on mine, sending a shiver through me. All I wanted to do was wash myself quickly so I could sink my dick deep inside her. But she wouldn't appreciate my eagerness. Her gaze followed my hand down my stomach. She swept her tongue across her lips as I went past my belly button. Her breath came in heavy pants, shooting excitement through my body, moving my hand towards my dick.

Her hand shot out and grabbed my wrist. "Not there."

"What?"

"I don't want a mouthful of soap."

She sank to her knees.

"Wha—"

She peered up at me as she took my dick in her mouth.

"Fuck." I grabbed at the wall and tried to find the soap holder. I shoved the soap in the general direction and missed. It thudded onto the floor. Taylor tightened her lips, gliding along my length. She twirled her tongue around the head.

"Fuck my mouth, Ciaron."

I nearly exploded on the spot. My legs were as weak as they'd been the first time I'd ridden a horse.

She wrapped her lips around me again and moved her hands to my hips. I curled my fingers around her head and pumped into her mouth. Holy fuck. She groaned and the vibration ran through my dick.

My hands tightened. I was conscious of not hurting her. I knotted my fingers in her wet hair, trying to get some purchase. The suction of her mouth increased. A small gag escaped as I pumped a little too hard. Without missing a beat, she adjusted the tilt of her head.

My fingers squeezed as the pressure inside me built. My legs tensed. She sucked harder. I exploded inside her mouth. My dick jolted as I kept hold of her head.

"Fuck." I could barely breathe.

"Fuck." I let go of her head and grabbed at the wall, willing my shaking legs to support me.

Taylor disengaged her mouth from my dick and stood. Her tongue darted up my chest and across my collar bone before she sucked on my neck, sending another tremor through me.

She whispered in my ear, "Kissing and making up is fun."

∼

I WOKE with Taylor wrapped in my arms. It was in these quiet moments in the morning I'd think about our future. At the beginning, when my arm was around her, the thoughts were all positive. Then, as we'd drifted apart in life and in bed, they became tainted. Now, as I lay here, they were hopeful.

I wasn't ignorant of the fact that we had a long way to go. A few sincere discussions and some hot sex wasn't going to fix all our problems, but they were a good start. And not just for me. Because every positive step in our relationship was a positive step for the kids. The changes she made were for all of us. The problem now was sustaining them. I needed to step up too. I needed to be the man she'd married. The strong one. The one who would do everything he could to keep her.

Before, I wasn't sure she'd ever change. She hadn't made any effort after we'd split. Most other people would have panicked and held on tight. She'd actually seemed to get worse. Now it was the total opposite. It was as if a switch had been flicked. But a switch could be flicked off just as fast.

Taylor moved beside me and stretched. I kissed the top of her head. She gave a contented sigh.

"You should have a girl's day," I said. "Go buy a dress for this party."

Her eyes met mine. "Isabelle would like a new dress. I'm sure we can find something that won't break the bank. Or maybe we can get a couple of new accessories instead."

The drought meant we were always watching our money. We'd had so many plans for improvements around the farm, including my taking a university course in pasture management. All we knew had been passed on. We'd thought it was important to get some science behind it. But all of that had been put on hold. And as much as I knew

Taylor tried not to dig into those savings, it had been unavoidable. Taylor would be thinking that a dress was a frivolous expense. And she wasn't wrong.

"Isabelle loves op-shopping," I said.

"Do you think your mam will enjoy a day out with us?"

"Yes, she'll love spending the day with Isabelle."

All I could hope was that she would play nice. She seemed to push Taylor's buttons a lot.

"OK. I'll ask Isabelle."

"A new dress, a day off school, time with you. I doubt she'd say no."

Taylor kissed me softly. "Thank you for your support. Will you be OK to cover my jobs today?"

"Shouldn't be a problem. The feed runs will take a little longer and I can shuffle a couple of people around. One day won't kill us."

She rolled out of bed. "I'm going to see if Isabelle's awake."

I sat up and swung my legs out of bed. "Looks like we won't be kissing and making up this morning."

She smirked. "I was just thinking of your well-being." She leant down to kiss me.

"Getting it on three times in twenty-four hours might be a bit much for you."

"Nice of you to care."

"Rest up for later. I'm going to see Isabelle."

And with that, she was gone. My dick may have been disappointed, but my heart was happy. She was excited to spend time with Isabelle and she'd said 'later' with such confidence I had no doubt we were on the road to recovery.

22

Taylor

Ciaron was right. Isabelle jumped at the chance to go dress shopping. And Mum and Mary were all too happy to join us.

"It was so good of Ciaron to give you the day off," Mary said.

I gripped the steering wheel. She didn't say how good it had been for me to give him a day off. "The whole day was his idea, actually."

And I loved him for it. Every day, I loved him more. I'm sure he had doubts about whether we could make it work, but not once did I feel them from him. Every day he gave me more. And when I'd told him how my talk had gone with Isabelle, he'd reminded me that actions speak louder than words. And he hadn't been accusatory. He'd simply said it to help me, to help us.

"Ciaron has always been a good boy. Always helpful and caring. That's how you met, wasn't it? He thought you needed saving?" Mary said from the backseat.

I rolled my eyes and then noticed Isabelle watching me in the mirror. I held my tongue, like always. Ciaron did save me that day because of the person he was, but that wasn't why we'd met. He didn't look at me and think I'd needed saving. And I didn't beg him to help me. I wasn't some damsel in distress. Unlike her. How many days did she cry when he was leaving, begging him to stay because she couldn't do it all alone? Perhaps she should have thought of that before she'd had so many children to all those different men who couldn't, or wouldn't, step up to the father plate.

How many times had Ciaron been both father and mother to his brothers? When he was just nine, she'd left him alone to look after his one-year-old brother Seamus for weeks. She'd left a nine-year-old to look after a baby. She did the same with Ronan, Billy and Tommy. Ciaron had looked after all of them. And not just on her little trips away, but when she was home as well.

There was no way in hell he was going to let those boys be taken away and separated. He got smarter each time. He'd hide food in the back of the cupboard so they could eat in the time she was away, and he took small amounts of money and put that away too. He was a fucking child looking after children while she went out and had a good time.

He gave those boys more love than he'd ever received. And never received any recognition for it. She'd never thanked him. Nothing.

I needed to let it go. Being judgemental was not helping me.

I took a deep breath and let the silence stretch out. It would be safer if I didn't answer.

Isabelle faced Mary. "They didn't meet because Mum

needed saving, Mamo. But Mum fell in love with Dad because of it."

Twice in two days she'd stuck up for me. I don't know if she'd read her Mamo's intentions or whether she was simply saying it the way it was, but it was reassuring. It gave me hope that she saw the good in me. I don't know if Mary never saw the good in me because she was threatened by me or she thought I wasn't enough for Ciaron. I didn't have the same issue with his father.

Ciaron and I walked into a large room with grey chairs and tables bolted to the floor. He guided me to a table where a man sat on his own wearing a white t-shirt and blue pants. There were other prisoners in the room dressed similarly. Three guards were standing near the walls.

He looked up and smiled and it was like I was looking at an older Ciaron—same brown wavy hair with a decent amount of grey, cheeky green eyes but surrounded with wrinkles, lips that quirked the same way as Ciaron's. He glanced between Ciaron and me, a smile emerging.

He stood and embraced Ciaron. "Son, so good to see you."

His accent was one of the strongest I'd encountered. Before Ciaron had a chance to say anything, his dad pulled me into a hug and said over my shoulder, "And who is this beautiful cailín?"

"I'm Taylor. It's nice to meet you, Mr Murphy."

"Call me Patrick."

So far this was so much nicer than meeting Mrs Murphy. Ciaron had warned me that even though it was a low security prison, visiting rules were tough. We weren't supposed to have physical contact with the prisoners, but neither Mr Murphy nor the guards seemed to care.

He let me go and cocked his head. "Where are you from then?"

"Australia."

"Sit. Sit. Tell me everything. Tell me about the lady who is about to steal my son away."

I considered him. How did he know that?

He grinned. "When you spend time inside these boring walls you learn to notice things."

Ciaron and I sat next to each other, holding hands.

"First, Ciaron has never brought a girl here before."

Ciaron's grip firmed on my hand.

"Second, Ciaron has a new tattoo, a Claddagh, with your name in it."

Ciaron glanced at his wrist.

"Serious stuff a Claddagh. Next, you are not only beautiful, but brave. You weren't scared of my arms around you."

"Ciaron wouldn't ask me to meet you if it wasn't safe."

"Aye." He pointed to my hand, which was wearing a Claddagh ring. "Serious stuff."

We spoke about how we met, and Patrick hung onto every word.

"When are you leaving, son?"

"As soon as I can."

Patrick nodded, his eyes solemn. "Does your mother know?"

"Aye."

He kept eye contact with Ciaron. "This cailín is your future boy. Do not let your mother take this from you."

"I won't, Dad."

Patrick knew exactly what Mary was like. We found out later the only reason he went back to her every time he was out of jail was for Ciaron. He wanted him to have a father, well, the best father he could be, and wanted him to have freedom. He didn't go back after Ciaron left.

As we walked into the first op shop, Mary said, "What are we doing at a charity shop? I thought we were going dress shopping."

"We are Mamo," Isabelle said. "I bet we find some good ones here."

Mary's eyes narrowed. "I can buy you a new dress if your mother doesn't have money."

Did she have to be so condescending?

I looped my arm through Isabelle's. "Isabelle likes shopping at op shops. She often finds things you can't get anywhere else."

Mum followed behind. "I think what you're wearing now came from here, didn't it, Isabelle?"

Isabelle nodded. The skirt and top she was wearing were a sweet, flowing boho style. It matched her hair, which was haphazardly braided. I had no idea how you could make hair look so messy but perfect.

"Oh yes, that's lovely," Mary said.

By the time we'd finished at the third op shop, Isabelle had two dresses and a few other things. She'd chosen a dress for me that she declared her father would love because it was an olive green like the hat I wore the day we met. Mary neither agreed nor disagreed, although she had an almost imperceptible sneer. She didn't buy anything on the premise that her suitcase was full already.

We finished off our outing with a late lunch of sandwiches at a local park. Although we hadn't spent much at the op shops, I didn't want to spend what we could save. A simple lunch was our best option. In good years, we would have gone to a local winery, but this was not a good year.

Mary didn't say anything; although I had the feeling she was less than impressed.

Well, she could stay that way. I wasn't here to impress her. I was here to rebuild my relationship with the man I loved and the children who were my everything. I hung on to Patrick's words about not letting Mary take our future away from us. Ciaron had been strong enough over twenty years ago, and I would be strong enough now.

23

Ciaron

As soon as I opened the front door, the smell of Ireland hit me in the face. My mouth watered. I'd recognise the smell of Dublin coddle anywhere. It was a staple meal I made for my brothers when I was a kid. Cheap and easy was always my go to when making us food.

"Ciaron, my boy," Mam called from the kitchen. "I've made your favourite."

"Thanks, Mam."

She beamed at me as I walked into the kitchen and looked into the pot of roughly sliced pork sausages, sliced bacon, onions and chunky potatoes in broth. Some people might say it looked unappetising, but they have no idea what they're talking about.

"I browned the sausage and bacon just the way you like it," she said. "And made you some soda bread."

I smiled. I loved the dense texture and tangy flavour of soda bread.

Taylor was watching us from the lounge room where she was folding washing with the kids.

Mam cupped my cheek. "Nothing is too much for my favourite son."

Taylor looked down at the clothes in the basket.

"We need to keep the Irish traditions strong in my grandchildren. These Australians don't understand tradition. They eat anything." She shook her head. "Spag bol."

What was she even talking about? Irish people ate Italian food all the time. Lasagne was great comfort food.

"I'm going to get changed. Isabelle, Callum, can you help Mamo set the table, please?"

"No need. They have been helping *Taylor* all afternoon. Let them rest." Mum ushered them out of the lounge room and to the dining table, leaving Taylor to finish folding the washing. Taylor said nothing as Mam spoke to them quietly while setting the table. It was nice that Taylor let them have this time together.

When I came back out, the table was set, and the food served.

Mamo patted the chair next to her. "How was your day today?" she asked. "Tell me all about it."

My heart lifted knowing that she was interested in what I was doing. Before she arrived in Australia, the conversation revolved around her or how I could help her. This was a welcome change. Perhaps being here, she could see how involved working on our farm was.

When I finished telling her about the day, she patted my hand. "Good, good. It sounds like your day was busy as usual and you didn't need to do much extra because Taylor was away."

In my peripheral vision, Taylor shifted in her seat.

"We were able to share the extra work around," I said.

"I think what your mam means is that you pick up most of the load already, so a few extra tasks won't mean much," Taylor said.

"Yes, exactly," Mam said, giving my arm a rub. She'd never given me this much credit before.

Taylor's lips lifted in a smile that couldn't be less genuine if she'd tried. She remained quiet for the rest of the meal. Was she unhappy about someone recognising the hard work I put in? That was strange, seeing as she'd mentioned it herself only the other day.

∾

AFTER DINNER I drove Mam home. Before she got out of the car, she said, "How about we go for a walk? I haven't spent time alone with you all day."

I turned the car off and joined her on the road. The night sky was black and dotted with stars, and the full moon lit our way. Mam smiled up at me as we walked aimlessly. In my childhood she was never interested in spending this much time with me. Was she trying to make amends?

"I enjoy spending this time alone with you. Taylor won't mind, will she?" Mam asked sweetly.

"Not at all. She will be happy for us."

"She doesn't seem very comfortable in my presence. I do wish I could be closer to her."

I glanced up at the tree line where it met the dark night sky. It wasn't only Taylor I needed to be braver with. "I think some of the things you say can be misconstrued. Like how you said, I do so much work. It made it sound like she doesn't."

Mam rested her hand on her chest. "Oh." She shook her

head. "That's not what I meant at all. I can see the farm is important to her. She seems to sacrifice a lot for it."

"We are all working hard. The drought has been very tiring."

She took my hand. "Of course, of course. I just worry about you. You look so tired."

I sighed. That was the truth.

"You are not young like you used to be when you helped me with the boys. You worked so hard for us all. I never thanked you for that."

I concentrated on my footsteps to help ground me in this moment. I couldn't believe I was hearing those words. That she was sorry for the past. That she truly cared about me.

"You need to take care of yourself more. I know you don't want to, but if you moved back to Ireland, I could help with Isabelle and Callum. Make it easier for you. I have more time now that all the boys have moved out."

"Thanks, Mam."

I didn't want to move. None of us did, but her words of support meant the world to me. We walked in silence until we reached the intersection and then turned around.

"I will apologise to Taylor. I didn't mean to hurt her feelings," Mam said. "She does seem quite fragile at the moment."

"That would be good, Mam. I'm sure she will appreciate it."

Mam rubbed my hand. "I don't want to cause friction between you. Taylor is so lovely. Even when I was unkind to her in the past, she never spoke against me."

Who was this woman walking next to me? She'd changed. It gave me confidence that Taylor could change too.

24

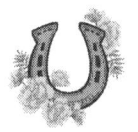

Taylor

I lay snuggled up to Ciaron in bed. "So work was OK?"

"Easy. It's not like you do much."

I poked him in the ribs, trying not to take his words to heart. "That's what your mam thinks."

He chuckled. "You and I both know that's not true."

"You could have told her so."

"I've told her before how much work you do."

"It would have been nice if you'd said it at the dinner table instead of going along with what she'd said."

"I spoke to her when I dropped her off. She said she didn't mean it that way."

"That's good." I didn't believe it for a minute. "I'm glad she said so." Let's see if she could manage to keep her snide remarks to herself from now on.

I needed to get off the topic of his mother. It wouldn't do us any good.

"Isabelle had fun shopping," I said. "Thank you for suggesting it."

"I knew she would. How did it go with Mam?"

And back to her we were.

"It was good."

It wasn't a complete lie. We'd been pleasant to each other, and she'd enjoyed her time with Isabelle. Ciaron didn't need to know that she thought we were cheap for buying second hand clothing. I didn't want to hurt him or his fragile relationship with Mary.

So, I'd played nice all day. And would continue to do so. Even when she practically accused me of being uncouth for cooking Italian food and insinuating I did nothing around the farm, that Ciaron practically did it all. Even though I knew exactly what she was doing, Ciaron didn't recognise it. He'd been so desperate for her validation his entire life and now he felt he was finally getting it.

She was as shifty as they come. She would play up to him, letting him hear what he wanted, while also planting a seed of doubt in his head. And that seed of doubt had my name written all over it. She had many more years of experience at this game, playing it for all Ciaron's life. The best thing I could do was stay quiet and not water that seed of doubt. I did not want Ciaron to feel like he had to choose between us. And the only way I could keep my cool was to remind myself she would be gone soon.

He held me tighter. "This weekend is our first weekend off together in just about forever."

"I feel a little bad letting everyone else do the work," I said.

"They only need to do the weekend feed run; it's not a full day of work. It won't add much time to their day."

I nodded. "True. We should do something together, the two of us, before the party."

Anything that didn't involve his mother.

He kissed the top of my head. "What do you have in mind?"

"We could go for a ride."

"You can ride me anytime."

"Is that so?" I ran my hand down his chest, his stomach, along the length of his dick. The little encouragement made it hard. This was much better than discussing Mary.

"Now would be good. You told me to save myself for later. It's later."

I threw my leg over him and straddled him, rubbing myself against his hard dick. The stimulation of my clit had it swollen in no time. Need spread through me.

"Like this?"

"Less clothes would be better."

He pulled at the hem of my pyjama top and lifted it over my head. Then he pulled at my bottoms. I manoeuvred myself out of them and sat astride him, naked. He was still fully clothed. It didn't seem to bother him though as he ran his hands down my side and rested them on my waist.

"You're gorgeous."

Tingles spread through me. After more than twenty years of marriage, he was still into me. And boy, was I into him. Every last bit of him.

Sitting up, he moved his mouth to my breast and sucked one and then the other. My nipples hardened in the cool night air. I ground myself against his hard-on and found the perfect friction point. My nipples were hard, my clit was hard and his dick even harder. I rubbed against him forcefully, enjoying his shaky breath on my skin.

I shuffled backwards and grabbed at his underwear, desperate to get them off, to feel skin against skin. My hand paused on the wet patch I'd left on the cotton. Ciaron yanked his underwear down and I nearly lost my balance.

I settled back over him. "You're a bit eager there, Irish Boy."

He smirked. "About as eager as your wet pussy."

I lifted a shoulder in a half shrug. "It knows what's coming."

His grin widened. "You."

Without a doubt.

I stroked myself against his length, my wetness making it slick. Then I took him inside me. Every centimetre sent another tremble through me and every tremble was amplified by his moans.

I slid up and down his length. His gaze roved over every inch of my body. Mine stayed glued to his face. His cheeks had a tinge of pink, which mirrored the heat travelling across my skin. His mouth opened with a rush of air, followed by a long, drawn-out moan.

Fuck, that was hot.

I moved faster. I tilted. The friction on my clit increased. Ciaron thrust inside me. Tension built. He stiffened underneath me.

"Fuck," he cried out.

He pulled me down hard. Tremors spread through me. Through him. He reached between us. As he jerked inside me, his fingers found my clit. The tremors turned into an earthquake.

I cried out and pulsated around him. All other movement stopped except me clenching as his dick twitched inside me.

"I love watching you come," Ciaron said.

I stayed on top of him as his dick softened. I was aware of the wetness between us, but I was too spent to move.

Ciaron held me firm and kissed me. Sex was as good as it had been twenty-two years ago. We were no longer in a dry spell. He helped me get dressed before we fell asleep with his arm around me.

I loved this man with my whole being. Nothing would separate us again. Definitely not Mary.

25

Ciaron

When I walked out into the kitchen for breakfast, Callum and Isabelle were sitting next to each other at the dining room table, chatting. They acknowledged my presence with sly grins before resuming their talk.

I wasn't sure what the grins were all about. I shook my head and started making pancakes. When Taylor entered and got the same grin, I got to thinking. Taylor helped me get the ingredients out. I grabbed her hand and pulled her to me before whispering. "What are they smiling about? Did you say anything to Isabelle about us getting back together?"

"No. I thought we were waiting. Although you did kiss me at dinner the other night."

I nodded, and she went to the fridge. When she came back, I said, "And then you kissed me back. But that was days ago. Maybe they heard us last night."

"When you showed me a good time?"

I chuckled. "Yeah."

She thought for a moment. "We weren't exactly quiet."

I nodded. "Should we talk to them?"

"Probably."

We finished making the pancakes and sat at the table with them. We were all quiet while we ate. I glanced at Taylor. Did she want to start?

Callum put down his knife and fork and considered us both. "Are you getting back together?"

I needed to play this cool and not over inflate it. "We're trying to work things out."

Isabelle mumbled something to Callum, and he laughed so hard he snorted.

"Is there something you'd like to share with us?" Taylor said.

Callum nudged Isabelle.

She giggled. "I said 'is that what they're calling sex now'."

Taylor bit her lip, trying not to laugh.

"A healthy sex life is important to a marriage," I said.

Taylor shifted in her seat. "Yes, well, anyway, your dad and I love each other, and we would like to fix what we broke."

I nodded. "It will take some time, but we're working on it."

"Good." Callum shoved a forkful of pancakes into his mouth and chewed with his cheeks puffed out.

It was good.

"Mum and I are going for a ride this morning. What have you got planned?"

"Nanna said she will help me with some decorations," Isabelle said. "Mamo can help too."

Callum shrugged. "I'll go with them into town. Make sure they buy good food, you know, chips and stuff."

I laughed as Isabelle rolled her eyes.

Taylor looked at her phone. "It looks like we have twenty coming with staff and friends."

"That's good. Not too big," I said.

Isabelle nodded. "Yeah. It was short notice, and school holidays have just started, so some have gone away."

Taylor poured herself some juice. "Before you go, can you strip your beds so I can put the washing on before we head out?"

They nodded. I smiled. Things were getting back to normal, back to where we were years ago. First, she helped fold the washing and now she was actually doing the washing. But not only that, she was invested in us as a family again. She was back on track to being the wife and mother she once was.

We finished our breakfast, dropped the kids off and headed out to the horses. Myrtle and Capall glanced at us. They had their ears forward, probably thinking they were going to get a second breakfast. When they saw we didn't have buckets, they ignored us.

"Bet Capall comes first," I said to Taylor.

"What are we betting for?"

Now, any other man who'd had a dry spell would bet on something sexual. But I was convinced getting more was a sure thing.

"Winner gets to help deliver the first foal."

"Deal."

Taylor climbed in through the fence.

I followed quick smart, then walked away from her. "Capall."

He swung his head in my direction

"Mrytle." Taylor raised her arms in the air.

Myrtle looked.

"Come on, boy," I called out. "We're going for a ride."

He nickered. I had him.

"Come on," I called in the tone all horses in the world responded to.

"Mrytle." Taylor had her arms in the air and started running on the spot.

Capall, being a gelding, had much more respect than the crazy mare. When he realised we were both calling, he cantered over.

"Good boy," I said, hugging him around the neck before giving him a treat. His soft muzzle brushed my fingers. I put his halter on and led him to the tack room.

Myrtle, on the other hand, ambled on over like walking slow was the competition. I laughed at Taylor's exasperated expression.

We saddled up and started along the side of the road toward the river. When I'd first arrived here, the paddocks were so vibrant it was like green on steroids. Now they were lacklustre at best, but mostly brown, and some paddocks were just dirt. Some days, I didn't even notice the desolate paddocks anymore; it was a part of our norm.

We'd had droughts before, but this was one of the longest. And there was no end in sight. The only thing I could tell myself was that with each day that passed, we were one day closer to rain. It didn't help the empty feeling every time I paid attention to the paddocks. But it did help to remind me that the drought wouldn't last forever. If not for that hope, what would be the point of going on?

I glanced at Taylor beside me. How many days had we spent like this early on, when days off were actually days off? Too many to count.

There was no grass here on the verge of the roadway. When it rained, we'd be mowing here every fortnight.

We were lucky we could still irrigate some paddocks. It was one of the reasons we had survived. The paddocks beside us still had horses - ten to a paddock.

Every horse on the farm had to be fed one scoop of feed morning and night, plus six bales of hay every day for each paddock. It all added up. If we weren't in drought, we'd only feed the pregnant mares half a scoop a day so they could get the vitamins and minerals they needed, and they'd eat grass the rest of the time.

The drought levy we'd introduced was another reason we'd made it this far. We'd had no choice; feed had quadrupled in price, and we couldn't afford to cover that.

So, the fact that we had client horses was a huge advantage. If it was just our horses, we'd be in a whole world of hurt. At least with clients, we still had some money coming in. It didn't mean it was easy to balance, though...just easier.

We walked past, heading to the river, lost in our own thoughts. For so long I'd wished we talked, and, in this moment, I was content not doing so.

I loved watching Taylor ride. She was so relaxed, moving seamlessly with Myrtle. I don't think any other rider could handle her sassiness and moods. Capall was more my type —chill.

Farmers were destocking all over the region. Horses, sheep and cattle. A one-year drought, farmers hedge their bets and feed their cattle. Two years and it becomes harder to sustain as prices of feed goes up. Agistment could be an option, but transporting horses to farms interstate was expensive. Next came destocking. They would start with the steers, move to the cull heifers and they would keep going, holding onto their breeding stock for as long as they could.

Same with horses. Breeding stock was what was important in the end.

Non-farmers didn't realise rain wouldn't be an instant miracle cure. It would take five years to recover from a drought like this. Five years for farmers to recover financially and rebuild their herds. We were lucky we were not at the stage of reducing the herd yet. Not every stud in the area had been that fortunate.

I took a breath. It was time to have the conversation we were probably both avoiding but should have had long ago. The fact that we hadn't talked about it had added extra strain to our relationship. We couldn't keep hiding.

Time to suck it up. "We need to talk about the drought and the farm."

Taylor's fingers tightened on the reins. She didn't say a word, only stared straight ahead. This was bullshit. Apart from our failed marriage, the drought was one of the biggest problems we'd ever had to face.

I squared my shoulders. "We should have spoken about it months ago."

She straightened her back. "I'm fully aware of that."

Mrytle's ears flattened back. Taylor must have tensed. She probably thought I was having a go at her. And if I had to admit it, in a small way, I was. Her closing me out still irked me to this day, even though I'd forgiven her for most things.

"Why didn't we?" I tried to make my voice gentle because arguing wasn't going to get us anywhere.

"Need I remind you that we didn't talk about much?" she retorted.

So much for us not having resentment. How much longer would it rear up for? I pressed my feet down into the stirrups as if I was preparing for a rough ride. We needed time to tame those feelings. This was one of those times I needed to speak up.

"No, you don't need to fucking remind me. Just like you don't have to bite my head off for wanting to talk now."

We walked along in stubborn silence. I lifted my hand to my face and squeezed my temples. This was getting us nowhere. I'd tried to be gentle. I'd tried to be firm. Neither had the result I wanted. Fucking hell. This was my fault.

"I'm sorry," I said. "I've stayed quiet for too long and now that I'm speaking up, it feels like an attack or an accusation or anything in between. It's not."

Taylor nodded. "OK. Let's talk."

I relaxed my legs and feet. Mrytle's ears returned to a forward position.

"If we don't get rain soon, we may have to sell some of the foals as weanlings instead of yearlings," I said.

Taylor sighed. "I know. We won't get as much money for them. We never do. They look scrawny compared to yearlings."

"We should probably consider selling a mare or two as well."

"I think we should see how we go in the January sales first."

My shoulders relaxed. "Agreed." Now for the big question. I knew my answers, but we needed to be on the same page. "What will we need to do to survive another year of this?"

"Keep some, agist some, sell some. That's all we can do. And I hate to say it... but we'll need to reduce staff again."

It's something I didn't want to hear, but it was the truth. We normally had ten permanent staff with four extra during breeding season. We were down to eight and two. I sighed. "It's so hard because they're like family and they have families and it sucks. Who would we even let go?" I couldn't, wouldn't, be able to choose. "Salty is the only one working in his family. His wife looks after his ailing mum. Cleo has been saving up for a new car. Fran is planning to have a baby. Rachel is still paying off the debts her husband left her. Everyone has something, everyone needs the money."

"It does suck. Have you started a list of the mares and foals and what you think we should do?"

"I have," I said. "But I think we should work through it together. We always make better decisions when we talk about things."

"Yes, we do."

I reached out and took her hand.

We rode like that for a while. And for a change, Mrytle tolerated Capall walking right beside her and touching her.

I was glad we'd at least started the conversation we should have had months ago. I was even happier that she wanted my input.

I sighed. "I'm sorry I didn't insist we talk about this sooner. It put all the pressure on you, and you would have felt unsupported." I rubbed the back of my neck. "That was unfair." As a result, she'd stopped asking for my input.

Taylor gave my hand a squeeze. "We're in a different place now. A better place, where we work on things together."

I smiled and nodded. She was right. There was more than just hope in my heart now, there was certainty for our future together.

26

Taylor

Ciaron and I got dressed. I paused as I watched him pull his jeans up his muscular legs and over his fine arse. When he pulled his green shirt on and buttoned it up over his chest, the sight was just as good. I loved how his wide, strong shoulders stood out.

"Are you going to get dressed?" Ciaron looked down at the dress in my hands.

"I got distracted."

He chuckled. "As much as I love seeing you in your underwear, we do have a party to get to."

I pulled the woollen dress over my head. It was form fitting at the top and flowed at my waist.

Ciaron let out a low whistle. "Isabelle said I'd be happy with the dress. That was an understatement."

He was standing in front of me within seconds. I couldn't believe I was jittery at his closeness. Another thing I'd taken for granted.

"You look stunning." He pressed his lips against mine.

"Thank you." I ran my hands down his chest. "I love this colour on you."

"Let's go before *we* get distracted."

He took hold of my hand and led me into the living room. Isabelle and Callum were already waiting, chatting to each other. Were all brothers and sisters like this or were they so close because they lived out here on the farm?

"We're going to have to start locking her up," Ciaron said.

Isabelle was wearing a navy and teal dress with long slits up the side which revealed her legs and cowboy boots. Callum, on the other hand, was so casual his shirt was untucked.

"You take the kids," Ciaron said to me. "I'll go get Mam."

"What about Nanna?" Callum asked.

"Dan said for this to be a real date he needed to pick her up and take her home," I said.

"Probably so he can get a goodnight kiss," Ciaron said.

"Do you think I can ask for an extra day's pay if he gets a kiss?" Isabelle asked.

Ciaron chuckled. "I reckon you could."

We left the house and went our separate ways. When I walked into the staff dining room with the kids, I gasped. There were fairy lights strung across the room and lanterns on the tables. The tables had colourful runners. When I looked closer, I recognised them as Isabelle's scarves.

"It looks so pretty," I said to her.

"It was Nanna's idea."

As we made our way to Mum and Dan, Ciaron and Mary arrived and joined us. Ciaron placed his arm around my waist, and I moved into him.

Dan's blue-grey eyes twinkled. "It's so good seeing you two back in the saddle. I didn't think your split would last."

"Oh really," Mary said. She snapped her mouth shut as soon as it was out. Then she took a small step back and studied us.

Mum's mouth dropped open, and she clutched Dan's arm, whose eyes widened at her reaction.

Ciaron and I tensed. Until that very moment, Mary had no idea that we'd separated. I broke out into a cold sweat as I tried to find my voice. It should have been natural for us to say thank you and we would have in any other situation. We would have been glowing. But as Mary's eyes narrowed, I wanted to be anywhere but here. I could never tell what she was going to latch onto to make my life more difficult.

"We're going to check the punch," Mum said before whisking Dan away.

I saw the moment she told him that Mary didn't know because he clearly said "shit" while throwing furtive glances our way. Mary watched the scene intently and then spun to Ciaron and me. Her lips were in a tight line. Ciaron shifted from foot to foot. Mary opened her mouth, presumably to say something. I stood ramrod straight, widening my eyes at Ciaron, inviting him to speak.

"Wow, this is amazing," Rachel said as she walked into the dining room. Thank God, it stopped Mary saying whatever she was going to say. Rachel made her way over to us and handed Isabelle a gift. "I love that dress, Isabelle. Happy birthday."

Mary's eyes were still pinned on us. My shoulders relaxed as I moved my attention away from her. Another person walked in. Someone I didn't realise we'd invited—the American vet, Curtis. He saw Rachel and smiled. That man could have stepped out from a modelling magazine with his wavy blonde hair and square jaw. And his teeth were perfect.

"Mum invited him," Ciaron said, loud enough only for me to hear. "She said, and I quote, Reason A- It would give Dan someone to talk to if their date fizzled out."

Curtis waved to Dan and went over to say hello. Reason A seemed like it would be effective.

"B - it would be good for Isabelle to interact with him before going on work experience because when he's working, he has resting bitch face."

I laughed. "Ain't that the truth."

He'd been loosening up slowly. He'd even started to laugh at Australian humour.

"And C,"—his voice dropped lower—"which she seemed to think was pretty important, he likes Rachel, and she needs to date because she hasn't since her husband died."

Curtis made his way over to us. Rachel clutched her hands in front of her.

"That's a lot resting on one man's shoulders," I said.

"Lucky he has no idea."

All the while, I could feel Mary's eyes boring into me, even while she had a conversation with the remainder of the group. Great. The longer she had to think, the worse it would be.

Two teen girls and boys turned up. Ciaron took my hand and led me over to the mother who'd dropped them off.

"Hi, Ciaron."

"Thanks for bringing the kids, Audrey. This is my wife, Taylor."

He'd called me his wife. I glowed. I wanted to hug him. Anyone would think I was a lovesick teenager.

"Nice to meet you," I said.

"Thanks, you too." She smiled. "What time do you want me to pick them up?"

"Eleven would be great. You're welcome to stay," Ciaron said.

"Thanks. I have a date with a book. My husband is away and without the kids in the house, I might get some peace."

"Enjoy," I said before she left. "I can't remember the last time I read a book."

Some other staff arrived and wished Isabelle happy birthday. They milled around, talking to each other. Before Ciaron and I could join Mum, Dan and Mary, I got a text.

"Pizzas will be here in ten," I said.

Ciaron nodded. "I'll let Callum know he'll be needed soon to help me pick them up at the gate."

I started walking to the others. Before I reached them, Mary cut me off. My stomach sank. I glanced at Ciaron. He was busy talking.

"I thought something was up," she said. "You can stop pretending now."

"We're not pretending."

She moved around and I was compelled to follow her, meaning I couldn't see Ciaron anymore. I couldn't make eye contact with him and ask him to save me. Why didn't he say something to her when he had the chance? Now I had to put up with her shit.

"Ciaron won't save you." How did she always know what I was thinking? Her coy smile made my stomach reel. "You couldn't hold his interest after all."

Our sex said otherwise.

I kept my mouth shut. She knew I wouldn't fight back. I didn't want Ciaron to have to choose.

"Do you really think you can win him back after you hurt him so bad?"

Had Ciaron told her? Surely not. I clenched my teeth, and she saw it. She knew in that moment that I blamed myself. She could always read me, and I hated it. I wiped my sweaty palms against my legs.

But it wasn't just my fault, I reminded myself. Ciaron had lost his way in the marriage, too. Jeez, imagine if I said that to her. I clamped my mouth shut.

"Did you get back together to spite me?"

I swallowed. It was better not to engage. Especially tonight at Isabelle's party, in front of everyone. If I started, I might not stop. I started to walk away, but she grasped my arm and reached out and tapped my cheek. I cringed. "Oh Taylor. A mother's love always wins. I have a week left. He *will* come home with me."

I shook my head. "He won't leave Isabelle and Callum."

"Maybe not, but he will leave *you*."

She laughed, pretending we'd had a lovely talk together, and went over to Isabelle and her friends.

I was left all alone, trying to control my racing heart and erratic breathing. Ciaron was gone. Why had he left me alone with her? Because I never told him what she was really like, that's why. Fuck me dead. This, what happened tonight, proved my suspicions. She hadn't changed.

I went over to Mum, Dan, Rachel and Curtis and tried to join their conversation. But I couldn't concentrate.

Ciaron and Callum came back with the pizzas. I went to help open the boxes and lay them on the table.

"What were you and Mam talking about?" Ciaron asked.

"Nothing."

Ciaron glanced sideways at me. I walked to the other end of the table. Now was not the time to discuss how awful of a human being his mother still was.

"It's not as bad as I thought it would be having her here," he said, smiling. "She's changed."

He was happy, and I'd have to rip that away from him. I didn't want to.

It wasn't just that, though. The bitterness Ciaron and I had felt today was bad. And if I told him what I truly felt about his mam, it could be worse than that. What was I supposed to do? There was no choice. I had to tell him. The question was, how?

All I wanted was for her visit to be over and her looming threat to disappear along with her. Then we could continue to mend.

As long as she didn't ruin it all first.

27

Ciaron

We sat around the table at brunch, talking about the party. Everyone seemed to have had a good time.

"Did you give Dan a goodnight kiss last night, Nanna?" Isabelle asked.

"Adults don't kiss and tell," she said.

Isabelle and Callum looked pointedly at Taylor and me. I rolled my eyes. It's not like we'd kiss and told. We'd only forgotten to use our 'the children are home' sex voices. After they'd mentioned it, we'd tried not to be so loud.

Taylor's phone rang. She got up and grabbed it from the bench. "Excuse me." She took the call outside. When she came back in, she said, "Sorry, I need to go. An owner called and said he's in the area and would like to visit."

"Do you want to finish your brunch?" I asked.

"No. I'm going to head to the office and familiarise myself with our breeding suggestions before he arrives." She leant down to give me a kiss. "I'll be home as soon as I can."

I watched as she headed out the door and to her car.

"Do owners normally visit on a Sunday?" Mam asked.

"Owners like to visit any time," I said.

"And Taylor always meets them? Even if you are doing something as a family?"

The kids shifted in their chairs.

Lorraine looked at Mam directly across the table. "When you own a business like this that relies on clients, especially during a drought, you make time for them whether it's convenient or not."

Mam nodded. We finished our brunch, and the kids made themselves scarce.

Lorraine stood. "Thanks for brunch. I've got some things to do today. Enjoy the day together."

I got up to wash the dishes.

"I thought the dishes were Taylor's job," Mam said.

"Usually, yes."

"Why don't you leave them, and we can go for a walk?"

I shook my head. "Taylor is at work. It won't hurt me to do the dishes."

She patted my cheek. "You're such a good boy." She followed me to the kitchen and started sorting the dishes for me. "What about all the times she works late? Do you cook and do the dishes then?"

Before we'd split up, the answer had been yes. But she'd been better since we'd gotten back together. Her priorities had changed. Mam was staring at me, waiting for an answer.

"She doesn't really work late anymore."

"Mmm."

An unfamiliar electric car drove past the house. The owner, I presumed. Mam and I finished the dishes and left the house to go for a walk. The maiden paddocks were beside us, and I watched as three of them ate hay under the shelter.

"How long did you and Taylor split up for?"

There was no point lying.

"Two months."

"And you got back together when you knew I was coming?"

That was a leading question. "Yes, I guess the two coincided."

"You don't think she will go back to the way she was before I got here?"

"No." At the start I had worried exactly about that, but I wasn't as concerned anymore. "Is that what you were talking about last night at the party? Our separation?"

Mam nodded with exaggerated head movements. "Yes. Yes. I was telling her how happy I was."

I smiled. "Thanks, Mam."

We continued walking, stopping every now and then so I could point something out to Mam. Half an hour later, when we were heading back home, the owner drove past us. When we got home, I expected Taylor to be there. All she had to do was meet with the owner and he was already gone. I shrugged it off even though Mam's lips were a thin line. One small thing didn't mean she was falling back into old habits.

But it took another half an hour for her car to pull into the carport. I couldn't ignore my sinking heart and Mam's 'I told you so' look. When Taylor put her keys on the hook, Mam said, "That was a long meeting."

Taylor looked between us. "I went back into the office to get a couple of things done while it was quiet."

That made sense. Maybe she had to note down some info from the owner or he asked for something and she had to help with that while it was still fresh in her mind. Or was I making excuses because I was too scared to face the truth?

A frown tugged at the corners of Mam's mouth. "You should enjoy your first weekend off in months with your family."

Taylor's nostrils flared. "I'm here now," she said, beating me to it. "What would you all like to do? Watch a movie? Play a board game?" Her voice showed no indication of the irritation I'd seen on her face.

Mam looked at me. "A *mhuirnín*, what would you like to do?"

"Let's play Scrabble."

She smiled broadly. "You sit with your old mam and help her. Some Australian words may be confusing."

Taylor spun around. "Maybe Isabelle or Callum would like to help their Mamo. I'll go get them."

When Taylor was out of earshot, Mam shook her head and said, "One hour to sort out some paperwork. I don't think so."

I didn't reply. I didn't want to admit that she was right. I went and got the box of Scrabble off the shelf. Taylor came back with Isabelle and Callum. Mam arranged the seating so that I was sitting next to her and Taylor was at the opposite end. Fear had me wondering if our priorities had become opposites again as well.

～

I stood at the front of the morning meeting and let everyone know the plans for the day. "As you all know, my mother is here visiting from Ireland. I'll be here for the next couple of hours and then I'll hand over to Lorraine."

Everyone glanced at Lorraine and nodded. After the

meeting, I headed off with her. We went to the foaling unit to do a stocktake on the milk and colostrum in the freezer.

"You and Taylor seem to be in a good place," Lorraine said as she pulled the bags of milk out.

"I think so."

"Do you think so or know so?"

"At the moment, we are in a good place."

"Ciaron, stop being so cryptic."

"I don't know. She spent a lot of time at work yesterday and that made me doubt how far we've come."

"From what I see, you've both come a long way. You seem to have a deeper appreciation of each other."

I smiled. "We've been trying very hard."

"And Taylor has been home more and is sharing tasks at home, so the weight is more even," she said.

"Yes. Because she's home for dinner every night, she does the dishes so I'm not cooking *and* doing the dishes. And she's been doing cleaning and laundry."

"All I can see are positives."

I nodded. She was right. All of it meant she was spending time with us as a family. I had no reason to doubt Taylor's love or dedication.

"What about you, Ciaron? What have you changed?"

I wasn't sure that I'd changed anything at all. And that was a problem. "I told her that in the end I resented her because I was doing so much, so I started leaving the decision making to her."

But that wasn't nearly enough. A few hard conversations weren't all that was needed from me. I needed her to know she had my full support. I needed to make sure she wasn't feeling alone in our marriage or the business. I needed her to know that she was appreciated. Fuck, I was an idiot. Why was I leaving everything up to her?

I counted the bags and put them in date order.

"So, you're communicating better?"

"Yes."

Lorraine gazed at me over the plastic bags of milk. "Taylor seemed upset after talking with your mam at the party. What was that about?"

I cocked my head. "Mam said she told Taylor how happy she was for us."

Lorraine shrugged. "It didn't look like that from where I was standing."

I thought about what Lorraine had said while we finished checking. Mam had been smiling a lot when Callum and I got back with the pizzas. Taylor not so much. Mam had said they'd spoken about her being happy for us. But now I wondered what Taylor's quick reply and the way she wouldn't make eye contact really meant.

"You're right. I shouldn't have accepted that answer."

Lorraine nodded. "You need to learn to speak up more."

I ran a hand over my face. "I thought I had been."

Fuck.

I started handing the bags back to her, newest first, so they could go on the bottom.

"I don't think it's just about me speaking up. I think I need to question more and not accept answers on their face value."

Part of our problem was that I didn't question enough. I let things slide until they became problems the size of Clydesdales.

We finished packing the freezer. "Thanks for your help. I'm going to head off now."

"Have a good day with your mam and the kids."

"Thanks."

I walked out and called Taylor to let her know I'd

finished for the day. When she told me to have fun, she seemed less sincere than normal. Her relationship with Mam had always been strained. I thought it was just typical mother-in-law, daughter-in-law behaviour. I thought Mam had improved after I spoke to her about her comments. But it didn't seem to change Taylor's attitude.

28

Taylor

Ciaron had his arm wrapped around me. It was so warm and toasty in bed I didn't want to leave. I snuggled in closer. He tightened his arm.

"I wish we could stay in bed all day," I said.

"Me too."

"Maybe the next weekend we have off."

He sighed. "It's so far away."

I reached for his hand and raised it to my mouth, kissing it.

"What did you and Mam speak about at the party?"

I kissed each of his knuckles.

"I thought you had smoothed things over, but you were quiet afterwards, so that had me thinking." It all rushed out of him.

I pursed my lips. What exactly had she said to him? Did she spread doubt into his mind as well about his losing interest in me? The morning had just started, and she was already ruining it.

I turned around in his arms and found his lips with mine, ending the conversation before it even began. He pulled me in closer and then rolled on top of me. I opened my legs, and his weight redistributed. He clasped my head and kissed me with fervour. He rubbed his hard dick against me through my PJs. The pressure sent a needy ache through me.

I yanked at his sleep shirt and pulled it up. He drew away so that I could take it off. Then he helped me sit up and tugged mine off. The bed covers fell to the side and cool air kissed my bare skin. As we sank back down, his chest pressed against mine.

We kissed again and I swear kissing was nearly as good as sex. Nearly. His mouth was firm against mine. I was reminded again of how he owned every part of me.

Our lips separated and the cool air prickled. Ciaron kissed my neck, his mouth as eager there as it had been against mine. Lower still, kissing and grazing my collarbone with his teeth.

His rough hands held my side, pushing my breasts up. He took one into his mouth, his tongue pressing against my nipple. I moaned. The needy ache was increasing by the minute, and it was the strongest between my legs. He changed breasts, sucking on my nipple.

Mmm, didn't seem like he'd lost interest in me *at all*. And neither had I lost interest in him.

I pushed his shoulders down, eager for his mouth and tongue to be somewhere else.

He raised himself a little so he could look into my eyes. "Is there something you want?"

"What do you think?"

He shrugged.

Arsehole.

"I want you to go down on me."

He grinned. "I'm getting there."

He returned to my breasts, sucking my nipples and grazing them with his teeth. I moaned. He made his way further down my body and when he reached the top of my PJ pants, he kneeled so he could pull them off. I lay there with my legs spread and him kneeling between them, looking down at me, smiling.

He ran a finger through my wetness and dipped it into my pussy. "So wet for me already."

He inserted another finger and found my g spot. I raised my hips. He lifted the covers above his head. And lowered himself. Thank goodness, because I was about to force him there.

His tongue stroked up, sending a shiver through me. He had me so on edge it wouldn't take long. When it circled my clit, I pushed against his mouth, increasing the pressure. He took the hint and flattened his tongue out. I raised and lowered my hips, directing the rhythm.

A moan escaped my lips.

Ciaron inserted two fingers, finding the spot again. I planted my palms flat on the mattress. He groaned, sending vibrations through me. My hips tilted and Ciaron set his own rhythm with his tongue and lips. I squeezed around his fingers and cried out. My legs shook and Ciaran didn't stop until I lowered my hips.

The rest of my body was still tense. Ciaron kissed his way up to my mouth. His tongue repeating what it'd done between my legs. Another tremble ran through me.

He pulled away and grinned. "I think you forgot the-children-are-home sex voice."

"Again. Maybe you should remind me next time."

"I was kind of busy."

"Mmm."

He laughed. "As much as I'd rather stay here, they will be expecting us at the morning meeting."

I sighed. "I suppose."

I rolled out of bed and headed to the shower. It needed to be a quick one, so we weren't late. Ciaron obviously thought about being late too, because he didn't follow me.

∼

Ciaron had headed home mid-morning to spend the rest of the day with Mary and the kids. As much as I wanted to keep him to myself, it would be selfish not to let him spend time with his mam.

I hated to think about what she was saying to him. She'd said he'd lost interest in me. But his performance in bed this morning said the opposite. I'd told myself early into the relationship repair that it couldn't just be about sex. It wasn't.

Was it?

What was wrong with me? Why was I doubting everything? I'd let Mary get into my head.

When I got home at lunchtime, Mary and Ciaron were deep in conversation. When she caught my eye, she smiled. I tried not to overreact or overthink; they were only talking. People do it every day. Instead of joining them, I started to make lunch. When Ciaron came to help me, she moved onto the kids who were engrossed in their phones.

Even during lunch she would draw Ciaron's attention, talking to him quietly so I couldn't hear. What pissed me off was that he didn't even notice how hurt I was.

Now, I was sitting at my desk, avoiding going home. Because work was safer. And here I knew I was good enough. At home, I knew I wasn't. And this had been the problem for a long time. As the silence and isolation increased at home, I'd spent more time in my safe place. Textbook avoidance.

I stood up and shoved my chair back. I wouldn't give Mary the satisfaction of being right. I could change. I could be better. I had already. Why was I letting her get into my head? I was doing the best I could. Surely, Ciaron recognised that. He hadn't said so, but things were much better between us.

29

Ciaron

Taylor walked in as we were sitting down to dinner.

"Sorry I'm late," she mumbled as she sat down beside me.

The kids sat opposite, stone-faced. I'm sure they were thinking the same thing I was. We wanted to believe she'd changed, but she'd let us down. And this was the second time in a few days she'd done it. She was slipping back into old habits. We started eating in silence.

"Did another owner come in today, Taylor?" Mam said.

Taylor stiffened beside me. "No, Mary. I had a lot of work to do."

"Yes, I'm sure working in a business like this is hard. Maybe Ciaron can give you some pointers."

Taylor didn't acknowledge the statement. She stared down at her plate like it would tell her some deep, dark secret.

"I had a wonderful afternoon with Ciaron, Callum and

Isabelle. It will be so sad when I leave. I wish I could see them more often." She cupped my face.

"You have a passport now," I said. "You can visit again."

"I'm not as young as I used to be. I won't be able to do these long trips for much longer." She sighed.

I laughed. "You're not that old."

She stroked my hand. "It's always hard to admit your parents are getting older and reaching the end of their life."

Was she sick or something? Is that why she was different? More loving, like a mother should be.

"Are you sick, Mamo?" Callum asked.

"No. No. Don't be silly." Her laughter was a trill. "While I'm here, I'll need to teach you and Isabelle some Irish cooking so you can spoil your dad, seeing your mum doesn't cook."

The remainder of dinner was the same, with Mam filling in awkward silences. When we finished, Taylor collected the plates. I got up to help.

"I'm good."

The kids kissed Mam good night and went to their rooms. I took Mam home. When I got back, Taylor had finished tidying and was doing the dishes. I needed to talk to her about being late. We couldn't move forward with no communication.

I stood on the other side of the bench. "The kids and I were disappointed that you came home late tonight."

She scrubbed the pot I'd forgotten to soak. Her jaw clenched.

"Taylor?"

She glared at me. "Sorry for being late for the Mary show."

She finished the pot and practically threw it into the dish rack.

"What are you talking about?"

She scoffed. "Nothing, Ciaron."

I clutched the back of the stool. I couldn't believe she was jealous of my mother, who I hadn't seen in years. Was it because we were getting on much better now? I thought she'd be happy for me. Why did she think she could change but Mam couldn't?

"I'm sorry for enjoying my mother's company."

"You're so fucking blind." She huffed and threw the dishcloth in the sink. "I'll put the dishes away in the morning."

She stormed off to our room. She wasn't going to walk away from me this time. Or get away with not giving me honest answers. I matched her stride and grabbed her arm. She wrenched her arm away and whirled on me with a sneer.

"You were late after meeting with the owner too," I said.

"Keeping count, are you? Or is your mother doing that for you?"

"What is your problem with my mother?"

"I've got the problem? Not her? Fucking typical."

"What are you talking about?"

"She has done nothing but try to break us up from the moment we met. But you're so fucking busy trying to get her approval that you can't even see it."

My stomach clenched. She was delusional.

Her eyes were wide, wild. "I love *you*. Not everything you do for me. Can you say the same about her?"

Of course I could. She'd changed, hadn't she? Hadn't she?

Taylor's face was red and contorted. "She treats me like fucking shit, and you never speak up."

"What's there to speak up about?"

She threw her hands up in the air. "Nothing. She loves you. She's a fantastic mother."

I shook my head. "If she's so bad, why is she here?"

"Not of her own volition, is it? Our children had to spend their own money to get her here."

"She has four children to look after."

"Don't give me that shit. They're fucking adults. And when they weren't, who paid their school fees and brought them what they needed? It wasn't fucking her. It was us." She was shouting so loud I'd be surprised the whole farm couldn't hear it. "And who sat with them night after night helping with their homework over the phone and through email? It wasn't her, was it?"

I clenched my hands. "You said it didn't bother you that we helped them."

Her nostrils flared. "No, Ciaron, it didn't bother me. I love them." Her voice was like steel. "You're missing the whole fucking point."

The point? Yeah, my mam was the point. But what about *her* mother?

"Why did you tell Mum about what happened at the party but not me?"

"I haven't spoken to my mum about the party."

"Why did she know you were upset, then?"

"Because she's not fucking blind."

I stared at her, dumbfounded.

She was shaking. Her chest was heaving as she stared at me, waiting for something. And I had no fucking clue what.

"Open your eyes." She grabbed her PJs, stormed to the ensuite and slammed the door.

I waited for the shower to turn on. I got changed and hopped into bed. I squeezed my temples. What the fuck were they talking about at the party? Things were tense before that, but now they were at a whole other level. I needed to press Taylor about it...when she was calmer.

When Taylor came out, she slipped into bed without saying another word. Great. Looks like we were back to where we were two weeks ago.

~

My alarm went off, and I groaned. I hadn't slept well. I'd been thinking about the argument. I needed to get to the bottom of what Taylor meant. She obviously thought I was missing something. I went through all the interactions with Mam, over and over. Taylor was right. She had pointed out when Taylor had done things wrong, but that was because she cared for me, right?

But this wasn't the first time she'd tried something like that.

I was in our kitchen watching my brothers do their homework while I cooked dinner. Taylor was supposed to have called by now. I put the stirring spoon down and went to the phone. I picked it up to check if there was a dial tone. Maybe Mam hadn't paid the bill again, and it had been cut off. There was a buzzing on the line. It was working.

Mam walked in as I put the receiver down. "She hasn't called you today."

"No, she said yesterday that it might be late." I went back to the stove and stirred the stew. I grabbed a piece of meat out to test. It melted in my mouth. I turned the stove off.

Mam patted my arm. "She has probably thought about things now that there is time and some distance between you."

Here we go again.

"I'm sure she hasn't changed her mind. I haven't."

"She probably realises it would be better for her to have an Australian man. One that wouldn't need to leave his family."

I moved away, grabbing bowls and cutlery. "I will only be a phone call away."

"But we need you here. An Irish woman would be so much better for you. What about Molly at the pub? She's a lovely Irish girl."

"I don't think Molly is interested in men."

"Nonsense. Who wouldn't be interested in you?" She held a finger to her lips and gazed at the phone. "I know this feels all lovey dovey,"—*her voice had dropped to a soothing tone*—*"but I'm afraid you may lose interest. And then you will be stuck all the way over there with no one."*

"I love Taylor, Mam, and she loves me."

"Love can be so fickle."

I took her hands to reassure her. "It will be fine. I will be fine."

She looked at the phone. "Then why hasn't she called? If she loved you so much, she'd call."

WAS SHE DOING IT AGAIN, and I was just too stupid to see it? Taylor said she was. I needed to ask Taylor to work through it with me. To talk to me so I could understand it, not just about the jibes, but all of it, including the party. I thought back to the time she arrived until now, slowly putting the pieces together, but not quite believing them.

It couldn't be true. It was. Wasn't it?

Fucking hell. I was so desperate for my mother's love that I hurt the person I loved most in the world. I let Mam hurt the person I love most. I rubbed my face. I was a shit husband.

I opened my eyes. The bed was empty beside me. I

couldn't hear any movement in the ensuite or the rest of the house. This had never happened. Even when we were at our lowest. Yes, she'd come home late, but she'd never left for work this early.

I thought back again to the argument and about how she said she loved *me* and not all the things I do. All my life, until I met Taylor, I did everything I could for my mother and brothers. I guess I thought if I did everything right, Mam would love me. And maybe she'd stay home with us. She didn't.

As things started falling apart with Taylor, I fell into the same trap. I started doing everything again, taking on more and more. It was what I knew. It's what young Ciaron knew. It's how I made sense of the world.

I sighed and swung my legs out of bed. I didn't understand what was happening. Could we really be imploding this quickly, when things had been so good? But who was I fooling? A week and a half of good wasn't that great.

By the time I made it to the morning meeting, I had more questions than answers. And I was angry at Taylor for not explaining what she'd meant. And I was angry with myself for not already knowing.

Taylor was sitting up the back. She watched me closely, not smiling.

At the end of the meeting, Rachel stood up and addressed me. "We have all taken a vote. We've decided every time you think a sleeping horse is in labour, you need to assist with a flushing."

The room erupted in cheers. Everyone hated flushing mares—vets and stud hands alike. It could be messy.

I looked towards Taylor in the hope of getting help. Everyone else turned to see her reaction. But she was gone.

30

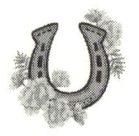

Taylor

Mum came into my office and sat opposite me. "Isabelle and Callum tell me you were late for dinner."

I clenched my jaw. "It's not a fucking crime."

Mum didn't bite back. "When I left at 3pm you were ready to leave too. What happened?"

This was bullshit. Why did I have to explain myself? I was a fucking adult. And I hated myself for disappointing my children. That's what pissed me off the most.

"What did Mary say to you the other night?"

Tears rolled down my cheeks. "She told me Ciaron had lost interest, and her love was more important than mine and she would take him from me, and it was my fault he left."

"Taylor! Why haven't you told Ciaron?"

I swallowed the lump in my throat. "Because he will choose her side." I sobbed. Mum rushed around the desk and hugged me.

"No, he won't." She hugged me tighter. "Is this why you've never told him how you feel about her?"

I nodded. Mum held me while I cried. "I did last night. But he can't see that she's a shitty person." I took in gulps of air. "He didn't believe me."

Mum smoothed my hair down and muttered, "That man. I'm going to kill him." She stepped away and took a big sigh, composing herself. "OK, tell me how that conversation went. Were you calm? Did you point out things to help him see?"

"No. I yelled."

"You need to *talk* to Ciaron. Face your fear."

She was right.

"Go home. Talk to him. I'll handle anything that pops up here."

"Thanks, Mum."

She gave me another hug. "Ciaron loves you. He will step up. If he doesn't, he'll have me to answer to. And then we can both divorce his arse."

I took a deep breath and nodded.

When I got home, I went in via the sliding door in our room, hoping Ciaron would be there, and we could talk. My shoulders slumped when I didn't find him. It looked like I'd have to drag him away from Mary.

Her loud voice carried easily down the hallway. "Garinion"—grandchildren, she was talking to Isabelle and Callum—"your mum can't help it. Work has always been more important to her than you."

I clenched my fists. It was bad enough she was trying to turn Ciaron against me, but bringing my children into it was low.

"It's not like that Mamo," Callum said. "She works hard, so we have a future."

"Nonsense. She couldn't even buy Isabelle a new dress."

I stormed down the hallway. Ciaron wasn't there. It was Isabelle, Callum and Mary. "Go to your room," I said to the kids.

Isabelle and Callum hurried out.

I spun on Mary, who merely smiled at me.

Bitch.

31

Ciaron

I paused my hammering and grabbed my next piece of scrap wood for the frame I was making for Isabelle. In the quiet I could hear horses in the paddock beside the shed whinnying and snorting. I never missed the sounds of the city with the constant traffic or the loud voices or the fighting. Whenever we went into the city now, I couldn't wait to leave.

Callum came running into the shed. "Dad, hurry."

My head jerked up. "What's wrong?"

He grabbed my arm and pulled me towards the house. "Mamo was talking shit about Mum."

"What?" My feet moved faster.

"Mamo was bagging Mum out. Mum heard. She's angry."

I broke into a run and charged into the house. Neither of them noticed me.

Taylor was yelling. "I've had enough of you. It's one thing turning Ciaron against me, but my children?"

Mam shrugged one shoulder. "It's working."

What the fuck?

"Why would you want to do that to me? To him? To your own grandchildren? Why would you want them to think they are unloved?"

"Not unloved," Mam said, smiling. "Just unloved by you."

Taylor stumbled backwards.

"Dad, do something," Isabelle begged.

I couldn't move. I couldn't process what was happening.

Taylor's reaction seemed to be what Mam was waiting for. Mam gave a small head tilt, which conveyed so much attitude. "I don't need to tell them what they already know. You're a terrible wife and mother."

"I'm a terrible mother? You left your children for weeks, months, at a time. And expected Ciaron to look after them."

Mum shrugged. "They survived."

"Do you even love them? Love Ciaron?"

Mam puffed her chest out. "This isn't about me."

Taylor shook her head, angry tears streaming down her cheeks. "I hope one day he can see through you."

Mam cackled. "Desperate men will believe anything. Like how I love him, and you don't."

"What did I ever do to you?"

Mam looked at her like she was the daftest person in the world. "He left me with those boys because of *you*."

"He left you with *your* children."

"For you. I have no idea what he sees in you."

"Why can't you just leave us alone?" Taylor's voice broke at the same time my heart did.

"That's enough," I commanded as I strode towards them.

"Ciaron." Mam rushed to me.

I dodged her and went to Taylor's side. Tears were

rolling down her cheeks. I clasped both sides of her face and made eye contact with her.

"You love us, and we love you."

Her tears continued.

"Taylor, I'm sorry I failed you. I'm such a fucking idiot."

"You didn't fail her," Mam said.

I turned on her faster than a racehorse leaving the gate. "I don't even know what to say to you right now."

"Say you'll come home with me."

Callum and Isabelle replaced me at Taylor's side.

I stepped towards my mother. "You are fucking delusional. Why would I ever go anywhere with you?"

"I'm your mother. I love you."

"You're not even half the mother Taylor is." My hands shook. "I was so stupid. All I ever wanted was your love. I thought you were different now, that you loved me. But the only person you love is yourself."

Her wide, pleading eyes hardened. "You're just like your father."

Once, those words would have hurt me. It would have felt like a rejection.

"My father did the best he could. He tried to be a good parent, unlike you." I turned to Isabelle. "Call Nanna. Ask her if she can come and pick Mamo up so she can pack."

Mam gasped.

I faced her again. "Taylor is my wife. I love her in more ways than I can even think of. A million times over, I would choose Taylor over you, every single time in every single life."

"Nanna is on her way," Isabelle said.

"Good. I'll take your grandmother outside to wait for her."

Mam stiffened her shoulders and walked out with me behind. Isabelle and Callum stayed with Taylor.

"After this, I don't want to see or hear from you again," I said.

Mam stared straight ahead.

"One day you might see that the way you treated me and the boys was terrible. I hope you do, because that will mean that you've found a shred of humanity."

Lorraine pulled up. I walked Mam to the car. Lorraine rolled down the window, and I rested my hands on the door.

"Mam has outstayed her welcome. Please take her back to your place to pack. I'll take her to the train station when she's done."

Lorraine shook her head. "I'll take her."

"Are you sure?" I asked. She shouldn't have to suffer because of my shitty mother.

"It's twenty minutes away. Better than driving her to the airport."

"Thank you. Don't give her any money. This is her own problem."

Mam flinched but didn't say a word.

Lorraine nodded. "How's Taylor?"

"She'll be OK. I'll make sure of it."

She rested her hand on top of mine. "How are you?"

"I have Taylor and the kids. That's all I need."

She squeezed my hand. "And you have me."

I smiled and stood back. Mum was the best mum I could have asked for. Her support for us was unwavering. She put her window up and drove away.

32

Taylor

Ciaron came back in and wrapped me in his arms. He was quiet for so long I wondered if he was ever going to say anything. I pulled away from the comfort of his arms and looked up into his face. The deep lines etched there made it look like he'd aged ten years in five minutes.

"I wish I'd seen it sooner," he said. "I'm sorry."

"I didn't know for sure. I only had a suspicion that she hadn't changed until the party."

He nodded. "Your suspicion was right."

"I didn't want the way I felt about her to cloud your relationship. I wanted her to love you like she should have."

He rested his hands on my shoulders. "All these years, you never told me how she made you feel."

I shrugged. "It didn't matter. We hardly saw her."

"It matters to me. You and the children are my world. It's my job to keep you safe."

My stomach dropped. That's all I wanted too. But not

telling him my suspicions wasn't keeping him safe. It led him to a world of disappointment. And why? Because I was insecure? Because I hoped I was wrong? Because. Because. Because.

"I'm sorry. If I had told you—"

"This is not on you, Taylor. There are a million things I should have done differently. I'm sorry."

I reached up and cupped his cheek. "You are loved by us, your brothers, Mum, everyone on the farm."

He nodded.

I stared into his beautiful green eyes. "I don't think she knows the meaning of love. Certainly not how you should love a child."

"But you do, Taylor. You love Isabelle and Callum completely."

"And you. I love you completely."

He bent his head to mine and brushed his lips against mine. "I will love you until my last breath."

I wrapped my arms around his neck as my lips met his. He grabbed my arse and pulled me against him and deepened the kiss. His tongue stroked mine. I smiled at the memory of our first perfect kiss.

"Ugh," Callum said.

Ciaron pulled away and grinned at him. "Isn't this what you wanted?"

"Yeah, but do we need to see it?"

Isabelle whispered something in his ear and they both burst out laughing.

Ciaron raised his eyebrows. "Something you want to share?"

Isabelle shrugged. "Just saying it's better than hearing your sound effects."

"Way better." Callum spun around and headed to the kitchen. "We'll cook tonight."

I pulled Ciaron back to me and kissed him with added sound effects. His response was to grab my arse and pull me closer with exaggerated moans and groans. I ran my hands over his back. When he hitched my leg up, I lost all composure and giggled uncontrollably. I peeked at the kids, who shook their heads and rolled their eyes. Then they smiled from ear to ear and gave each other a high five.

"We need to watch those two," Ciaron said. "They are a formidable force."

Just like us.

EPILOGUE

Two weeks later

Ciaron

I was sitting in my office, concentrating on my computer screen, when the two-way crackled.

"Are you on channel, Ciaron?" Rachel asked.

I grabbed the two-way off my desk. "Sure am."

"Mermaid is in labour."

"Coming."

I jumped out of my chair and jogged to the inner office. I didn't have long. Mares were not like humans; their labour lasts for around an hour. Some could be as quick as fifteen minutes. Taylor charged out of her office and crashed into me.

I shook my head at her. "She's mine. The deal was I got to help deliver the first foal."

She matched me step by step as I made my way to the ute. "You could at least let me watch."

I hopped into the ute and she did the same.

"I don't know," I said. "What do I get for sharing?"

"How about I let you live to see the next one?"

I chuckled as I started the ute and headed towards the foaling unit. "I was thinking something rewarding for the both of us."

"Mmm. OK. I can see how that would be your preference."

I rounded the corner to the foaling unit. "You better decide quick." I jerked the car to a stop and, in one fluid motion, turned it off and opened the door. I swung out of my seat.

"Shower sex," she practically yelled as my feet hit the ground. She opened her door before I even responded.

"Deal."

We jogged beside each other to the yard, not saying another word. We didn't want to disturb Mermaid or Rachel. The ground was wet next to where Mermaid was lying, where her water had broken. I made my way through the gate. Taylor closed it behind me. We didn't really need to be there for the birth, but the first birth was something to celebrate. Every birth was something to celebrate, and we had three months of births to look forward to.

Mermaid lay flat on the ground. Her stomach tensing and relaxing. The sack emerged, pushed out by two tiny feet that came next. Rachel was behind Mermaid. She grinned up at me as she reached for the bag and broke it with her fingers. Liquid gushed out. She took hold of the foal's legs and hung on. With every push, Rachel pulled and more of the foal's legs appeared and then a nose. When the mare rested, Rachel hung onto the legs, so the foal wasn't sucked back in. One last push and pull, and the foal flopped down onto the ground.

A perfect, wet, brown foal lay beside Mermaid. I glanced down at the foal slippers covering the hoof—soft rubbery tissue that looks like feathers or even tentacles. These little slippers protected the uterus and birth canal during pregnancy and foaling. Once exposed to the air, they start to dry and harden. And when the foal stands it wears/falls off quickly. To this day, even after more than twenty years of breeding, horses never ceased to amaze me.

I approached them and pulled the wet, slimy bag off the foal's head. Then I stripped the goop out of its nose. I helped it sit up on its chest. The foal's legs balanced it and the liquid I didn't get out dripped from its nose.

Rachel used the towel she had with her to clean the foal and stimulate its circulation. Mermaid stood and began licking it.

Taylor came and stood beside me, and I held her hand. New life was a miracle, a sign of better things to come. We waited. Rachel pulled the bag away from Mermaid and her foal and placed the ripped sides together to check that the complete bag had come out and the mare hadn't retained any. The jagged edges lined up.

The foal gathered its legs beneath itself. I held my breath as it wobbled its way to a standing position. It tried to take a step and fell over. I chuckled. We waited for it to try again. It did, and this time it remained standing. Then it made its way to Mermaid and started suckling on her leg. I chuckled. Foals are so dumb. Mermaid guided the foal to her teats, and it started suckling.

The three of us smiled.

New life. New hope.

Four months later

Taylor

Ciaron and I were mending a fence down by the river. Mermaid's foal had wandered down to see what we were doing. She was a funny little filly, always wanting to be involved in everything.

Thunder rumbled above us. The weather reports said to expect rain, but I didn't believe anything the weather reporters said any more. They'd been leading us on like a mare in season for months. Ciaron glanced up at the sky, then returned to tensioning the wire.

The wind had picked up, gusty at times, carrying dust from the bare ground with it. How there was any topsoil left after two years of drought was beyond me. I turned my back to the wind to protect my eyes. The leaves in the trees rustled. The foal ran back to Mermaid.

The horses were at the top of the paddock eating hay out of the hay feeders. They obviously didn't believe the thunder. It rumbled louder. A drop of rain hit my cheek. I stopped what I was doing and stood up straight, staring at the sky. More drops fell. Ciaron stood beside me and stared up.

Could this be it? The break in the drought?

Pounding sounded in the distance. The sky there was black but closer to the ground, grey as rain poured. It was loud, like a stampede of horses through a gully. It came closer. My stomach lifted. Just this rainstorm alone was more rain than we'd seen in years.

One rainstorm didn't mean the drought was over, but it would fill our tanks and turn the paddocks to mud, and then…then grass would start to grow again. We needed more, but this was the start.

Ciaron took my hand. Most people would run for shelter as the wind whipped at their hair and clothes. But not us. Not farmers who have been watching clouds appear and disappear for years. The drops hit us with more frequency as the rain approached. Then it was like we were standing in a shower. It fell straight down, not driven by wind.

Puddles formed around our feet. I gazed at the horses in the paddock. They turned their bums in the direction the rain was coming.

Ciaron wrapped his arms around my waist and spun me around. Tears mixed with the beautiful, fresh water ran down my cheeks. My feet hit the ground at the same time his lips crashed into mine. I held onto him as our lips moved and our tongues met stroke for stroke.

I couldn't imagine celebrating this with anyone but my best friend, the man I loved with all of my heart. The man who loved me with all of his.

∽

Thank you for reading Back in the Saddle. Would you like to share Taylor and Ciaron's first three days together in Ireland? Go here https://dl.bookfunnel.com/hstn7unxpo to see where their love story began.

The next book in the Diamond Firetail Farm series is Rachel and Curtis's story, Hitched for a Dream.
Click here to grab your copy.

Book reviews from readers like you are the lifeblood of authors like me. Reviews help readers find new books and authors find new readers. They don't need to be long and detailed, short and sweet are excellent too.

Please consider leaving a review in one of these places or anywhere books are celebrated.

Amazon

Goodreads

BookBub

KEEP IN TOUCH

To be notified of future releases, and to keep up to date with other news, please join my newsletter.
   https://www.subscribepage.com/p9p9y0

Diamond Firetail Farm

Hitched for a Dream

When my husband died, I was saddled with a lifetime of debt.

Enter Curtis, a brooding, no-nonsense American vet with a soft spot for horses. His proposal: marry him so he can stay in Australia and buy the business of his dreams. In return, he'll make my financial woes disappear.

It seems like a good business transaction to me. It's only a year of my life.

As we navigate life on the farm—from stubborn mares to nosy neighbours—I find he's not so surly after all. Beneath his gruff exterior lies a man who knows how to mend more than just animals. He can rescue hearts as well.

The problem? His constant reminders that we'll be free of each other in twelve months show his heart is not on the same track as mine.

At the end of twelve months my debts will be gone, but my heart may not survive losing the man I never thought I'd fall for.

Love Down Under Series

Novels

The Cat's Out of the Bag

Let Sleeping Dogs Lie

Get Off Your High Horse

Down The Rabbit Hole

A Bird in the Hand

As Busy as a Bee

Take the Bull by the Horns

Seal of Approval

Short Stories

In The Doghouse

Sealed with a Pooch Smooch

ACKNOWLEDGMENTS

Cover by Sarah Kil Creative Studios
Edited by Empowered Writing
Proofread by Half Caff Press
And thanks to my amazing beta readers

ABOUT THE AUTHOR

Cynthia is a Document Controls Manager by day and an author by night. She believes in happily ever afters and positive relationships. She enjoys writing about places she visited with her daughter while they travelled around Australia. She says that travel and reading are the best educators. A love of animals sees them feature in her books, some have small parts, others larger.

Find her online: http://cynthiaterelst.com/

All of her social links can be found here, Linktree: https://linktr.ee/cynthiaterelst

Manufactured by Amazon.ca
Bolton, ON